NEVER IS A VERY LONG TIME

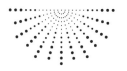

DONNA MCDONALD

Happy reading!

Donna M

WWW.DONNAMCDONALDAUTHOR.COM

ACKNOWLEDGMENTS

Thanks to my partners in writing crime, J.M. Madden and Robyn Peterman. You keep me honest and make me better at my craft. My writing journey would not be the same without you. Thank you!

Thanks to AJ for the edit and the advice on my fade-to-black approach. You are appreciated. Thank you!

Thanks to my readers for always giving my new work a chance. You really are the reason I write. Thank you!

DEDICATION

This book is for my readers.

THE PERFECT DATE SERIES

The essence of all romantic comedy is that falling in love and navigating an unexpected romance is never easy or simple. Instead, it's messy and emotional, and if you're lucky, it's also sexy and fun.

Some relationship professionals, like my character of Dr. Mariah Bates in this series, sincerely want to help people find their perfect love match. For the feisty heroines I've created, many of whom are older, Mariah's going to need all the help she can get.

Or maybe she just needs to step out of the way. You can be the judge.

BOOK DESCRIPTION

Cupid she's not—but she's pretty darn close.

Nothing in the world feels better than finding her clients the perfect date. Finding one for herself might be nice, but creative bill paying is not for accomplished doctors in their forties. Satisfied customers keep the electricity on.

Everything in her life was fine until she quit her celebrity radio job to start a dating business. Two years, a cheating ex, and a very ugly divorce later, she's back to living with her mother. Not that her mom isn't great, but come on.

With her cop ex-husband doing everything he can to ruin her business, she's at her wit's end. Throw in another cop who makes her want to believe in love at first sight again and life is a mess. Another sexy bad boy cop is the last thing she needs.

AUTHOR NOTE: I know it can be hard to know what's in a book these days. This is a contemporary, mostly clean, mostly sweet, romantic comedy with attitude. I hope this helps.

CHAPTER ONE

MARIAH FLINCHED AS THE WOODEN GAVEL HIT THE block in front of the judge.

"I'll hear from the defendant's attorney now."

Beside her, Bill rose and nodded once to recognize the judge's request.

"Your Honor—not to denigrate the fine work done by most detectives in our local police precincts, but the charges brought by my client's ex-husband, Detective Luray, are not backed by anything of substance. Dating services are a dime a dozen these days... no offense to my own client... but I'm having a hard time figuring out the grounds for the illegal solicitation charge the Prosecuting Attorney's office is attempting to press."

Mariah saw the judge look past her attorney to her. She was frowning and all but glaring. Dan wanted her to suffer for divorcing him and it looked as if he was actually going to get his way.

"Thank you, Counselor. Now I believe I'd like to hear your client's own defense of the charges against her," the judge declared.

"Yes, Your Honor." Bill leaned in. "Tell her your story, Mariah."

Mariah stood. "Your Honor, my name is Dr. Mariah Bates. I have a PhD in Psychology from Johns Hopkins. I am a licensed and certified marriage and relationship therapist. For over twenty years, I did a call-in radio show that helped people with their relationship issues. Now my primary business is an elite, professional dating service that is really more like a matchmaking service for busy professionals. We're a bit like Kellerher International, which is widely known, and as far as I know, quite well respected."

"If I might interject…" the prosecutor said loudly. "Dr. Bates's business does not offer access to a dating database of potential matches nor does she offer anyone a phone app as do most services of her kind. Nothing discovered in her business model indicates she is offering any ongoing match service, but rather she is selling individual time spent with a client to yet another client. It is reasonable to conclude that her business model is a potential cover for nefarious escort activities."

Mariah felt her jaw tighten. There had been no discovery at all. No one had subpoenaed her records. No, Dan had given the Hamilton County prosecutor all that misinformation. But who was going to doubt one of Cincinnati's finest?

"We charge a flat fee per service which translates in

most cases to a flat fee per date. The person we find the match for pays the fee, especially if there is a pressing need, such as a business function, wedding, or other social gathering where the client feels it would be best to have a companion at his or her side. We are not following the subscription model because of discretion. This is the same reason we don't use anything like an app. Our clients are CEOs, local celebrities, sports figures, and have other high profile jobs. We work to protect the privacy of every client we help."

She turned her head to the man seated several rows behind her wearing a very expensive suit she'd bought for him five years ago. It was easier today to ignore how good Dan looked in it. Her bitterness over his actions had torn away the rose colored glasses she normally viewed him through.

"As I have repeatedly told my ex-husband, Detective Daniel Luray, the way I bill is not proof of solicitation. Instead, it provides me a reasonable cash flow to continue serving my clients. Fostering twenty-two weddings among clients last year could be used as proof of my matchmaking success, if such proof is necessary. My clients are business people who would not appreciate their carefully selected date being called an "escort" for no good reason other than Detective Luray's unfounded suspicions or his desire to get back at me for having had the nerve to divorce him."

The judge looked at the prosecutor. "Is there any real evidence against Dr. Bates's company? Any client claiming they paid for sex and didn't get any? Anybody saying they're being pimped out by Dr. Bates?"

"Not yet, Your Honor, but…"

She didn't allow the prosecutor to waffle any further. The judge's gavel hit her wooden block. "Case dismissed due to lack of evidence. Dr. Bates, we are sorry to have wasted your time this morning."

"Thank you, Your Honor," Mariah said, breathing out at last.

Bill reached over and hugged her. "You could have mentioned me and Abby, you know. We're proof of your success and you didn't even have the agency then."

Mariah shook her head. "Dan's vendetta against me is no reason to drag my friends down into the mud. It's bad enough he has me wrestling around with him in it."

She gathered up her things and moved to walk out. Bill walked closely behind. She should have guessed it wasn't going to be that easy.

"One day I will get what I need for evidence, Mariah. I'm going to be watching your ass very closely," Dan warned as she walked by him.

"Great news. Kiss my ass while you're back there nosing around," Mariah ordered, striding away from the man she had loved forever but now loathed.

Behind her, she heard Bill say something to Dan, but it was probably best she not know what passed between the two men. All of her friends had taken her side in the divorce when her long time, nice husband had suddenly turned into an ass just because she quit a lucrative job to start a more risky one. Their loyalty to her had gotten even stronger after the divorce was final and Dan was seen around town with some yet to be named bleached-hair blonde on his arm.

Mariah huffed because crying over the sad state of her love life was out of the question. She was beyond emotional hurt now. That kind of hurt had come when she went off the air and decided to do something different because she needed to feel alive and not just on autopilot. The emotional hurt had come with the thousand arguments she and Dan had frequently had about their financial inequities and her earning power—the net result being a property settlement that left her literally homeless. Dan had come out of the divorce as well as any greedy, manipulating spouse ever could have. She'd come out of it stripped of half her wealth, but missing most of her dignity.

But the good news for Mariah was that the legal cords were finally all cut. That was what mattered to her these days. Now she could move forward the way she needed to. She'd been like a rabid, trapped wolf at the end of her divorce proceedings. She'd been willing to sacrifice an arm, a leg, and the nearly million dollar home she and Dan had bought with her celebrity earnings.

Setting the trumped up criminal charges she'd just faced aside, Mariah actually thought she *had* escaped. Unfortunately, Dan continued to be there on the edges of her life—still poking and prodding at a decision he thought he had some right to have an opinion about.

Why did he bother with trying to hurt her? She'd already given him the lion's share of their possessions. Her mind kept churning on the issue, but the truth was unknowable. When your once loving husband became greedy and spiteful, there was no more pretending you understood him.

When it came right down to it, there was only one

thing Mariah knew for certain these days. Divorcing Dan had put her off all men for a good long while. She could only hope her own sad relationship story wasn't going to be bad for her matchmaking business.

CHAPTER TWO

"Mariah?"

Mariah lifted her head from her laptop and the task she'd hoped would distract her from her woes. Dr. Della Livingston, her twenty-seven year old multi-tasking miracle who worked mostly in exchange for research data for her book, looked ready to have a meltdown. "What's wrong, Della?"

"I know you just got back from court, but there's a Detective Monroe here asking to see you. He says he was referred by someone."

"Oh, for pity's sake. I've had enough of this," Mariah said, rising from her chair.

She straightened her unfortunately super snug pencil skirt back down over her hips. Both pieces of her favorite suit had gotten tighter in the last couple of years, but it was still the best one she owned. That was why she'd chosen it to wear to court. The light shade of rose flattered her blonde complexion without looking too feminine.

Mariah marched to the door of her office. Taking one more deep breath, she moved by a still cringing Della, until she was standing in front of the still seated man. She glared down at him. "What can I do for you, Detective Monroe?"

To her annoyance, the man's face blushed crimson just at hearing her tone. His gray eyes briefly dropped down to her legs, but they didn't linger there long, before returning to her face. Good thing too. With that much gray at his temples, the man damn well ought to know better.

"Is that how you typically greet your prospective clients?" he managed to choke out.

"No," Mariah declared flatly. "It's how I greet sleazy cop buddies of my detective ex-husband who think they're going to come around and dig into my business for no good reason. The charges were dismissed today due to lack of evidence. You've got a lot of nerve showing up here."

"Uh… that's not why I came," he stammered out. Then his brow furrowed. "Who's your detective ex?"

"Don't waste my time with inane questions," Mariah ordered. She watched him reach up and run a nervous hand thorough his perfectly cut hair. Had the man really believed she'd accept his lame story? It would be just like Dan to plant someone as a client here to spy for him. Well, she was not buying this new detective's innocent act.

The man cleared his throat and stood, towering above her by a good foot or more even in her heels. Her gaze traveled up to his now pained-filled gray eyes. She glared until he finally looked away from her.

"I believe I made a mistake in coming here. Elliston said you were… well, it doesn't matter. Sorry to have bothered you."

"Elliston?"

"McElroy," he said tightly. "Geeky nephew of mine. Said you were fixing him up with the perfect woman."

Hands that had been fisted on her hips dropped to her side. "I will neither confirm nor deny to you that anyone is or is not a client of my business. Privacy is not just a buzz word I throw around. However, I appreciate all referrals. If this was an honest one, I'm sorry for jumping to wrong conclusions."

He studied her for a few long moments and Mariah let him get by with it. The silence helped to calm her.

"Bad day?" he asked.

Mariah nodded. Why not confess? If the man was lying to her, Dan had already told him anyway. "Nothing life changing, but I had to go to court this morning. The experience left me a little less trusting of anyone with the first name of *Detective*."

"I caught the gist of that in your greeting. Ex causing you problems?"

"Let's just say I'm not at my best at the moment, so this unfruitful conversation can end."

His almost bashful smile over her defensiveness did strange things to her insides. What she felt in the lower regions of her body made her mad at herself. However, if he truly was Elliston McElroy's uncle, she needed to be polite.

"Let's start again." Mariah put out her hand to shake. "I'm Dr. Mariah Bates—the owner, CEO, and general doer of every role here at *The Perfect Date*."

He stared at her hand for a split second longer than proper, then swallowed her hand with his own extremely large one. He didn't shake it so much as hold it for a moment. Mariah had to stop herself from wiping her hand on her skirt when he let go. "What can I do for you, Detective?"

"First name's actually John—not Detective," he said, correcting her. "And I'm thinking coming here really wasn't the best idea. Can we just pretend I wasn't here at all?"

Mariah rolled her eyes and drew in a breath. "Look, Detective Monroe..."

"John..." he corrected again.

Mariah sighed. "Look... *John*... normally I'd sit out here and talk you into feeling a certain comfort level before coaxing you into my office for a more private chat. Seeing as how I've already yelled at you and accused you of many things you profess to be innocent of..."

"Well, I..."

Mariah held a hand up. "No, no. That's quite okay. If I'm wrong, I'm wrong. I absolutely don't want you to dash away and tell the person who referred you that I was blatantly unkind. I normally am not unkind. I'm normally quite pleasant and supportive."

Mariah fought back a sigh when his grin made a single dimple on one side of his face. His gray eyes lit with amusement. All in all... he was quite handsome.

"Unkind?" John asked. "Is that a new way of saying you tried to hand me my balls over something some other guy did to you?"

"Yes, and you're a very wise man for understanding. Please accept that this is a rare, rare day in my otherwise drama-free life," Mariah answered.

"Sure. I promise I will never tell anyone you were unkind to me," John promised softly, grinning still.

"Good. I wish you'd change your mind then. If you stay and talk to me, I promise to do my best to find your perfect date."

Head down and grinning even wider, John shook his head as he walked to the door. He raised his gaze to meet hers as he prepared to leave.

"I bet you could find her easier than you know. Good day, Dr. Bates. Maybe we'll run into each other again. Maybe I'll find my balls and come back. Anything is possible."

Mariah chuckled and felt her face heat. Lord, what had she done now? "I'll be more gentle with you next time," she promised, shocked to hear the flirty statement escape her mouth.

Laughing for real, John exited. Mariah turned to go to her office and saw Della still staring at the door. "What are you pondering, Dr. Livingston? The fact that I screwed up with a potential client, or the fact that I just went nova on a man in front of you?"

Della shook her head. "Actually, I was wondering how in the space of five minutes you went from yelling at Detective Monroe to flirting with him. Also, I'm 99.9% confident he started the flirting part of the exchange with his balls comment. I feel like I should be taking notes, but I wouldn't know where to catalog what just happened."

Mariah waved a hand. "What you witnessed was two mistakes clearing up awkwardly. Detective Monroe was never going to let me help him find a woman. Which is just as well because I'm not sure I could have matched up a still working detective without advising the woman to run away as fast as her legs could move. It's oddly fortunate that I ran him off because now I don't have to worry about my conflict of interest. It was a fairly charming end to a less than charming problem."

Della chuckled. "I'm pretty sure that was a beginning, not any kind of end."

Rolling her eyes at her young assistant's dreamy gaze, Mariah headed back to her office.

SHOULD SHE TELL HER LAST CLIENT OF THE DAY THAT his alleged uncle had come by to see her? No, of course not. What if the man hadn't revealed his intentions to his nephew? There was no reason to compound her professional sins.

Pushing away thoughts of the grinning John Monroe, whoever he really was, Mariah studied the man leaning forward in his seat. He sighed at nearly every picture he saw.

"Problem with my choices for you, Mr. McElroy?"

Elliston McElroy, a successful entrepreneur who made software apps for a living, didn't answer her question immediately. He lifted and held up his swiping finger briefly before returning to his task of looking through the women on the tablet she'd handed him.

According to his worksheet, Elliston was five-foot ten, but he carried himself like he was six-foot eight, a family trait probably since the uncle was over six-foot tall.

His close-cropped, light brown hair was gelled to stand

straight up on top. The spiked hair, along with the tribal tattoos running down both forearms to his hands, created a European Soccer team look.

Despite the faddishness, he pulled off the dress clothes he wore well. The sleeves of his well-made pressed cotton shirt were rolled casually to his elbows, no doubt to show off the tats.

Mariah thought his thirty-two year old character was mostly revealed in the clear, blue-eyed gaze he turned her direction just before he spoke.

"Please call me Elliston. I can't handle the mister stuff. The women you picked for me are all very beautiful," he said at last.

Mariah shrugged. "We do mini-makeovers to help each client present their best for our catalogue. It helps that most work out and keep themselves maintained. I often tell male clients that we enhance female clients for presentation purposes only. Most do look a lot like their photos. I find people don't like physical surprises about their dates."

When Elliston sighed again Mariah lifted an eyebrow. "You're sighing very heavily. What's wrong with them?"

His grin over her understanding was very arresting because his real masculine beauty showed up in it. Any woman would be thrilled to see that smile on his face every time she came into view.

Elliston wasn't classically handsome with all those lean angles to his face, but he had that something special that made a woman want to stare at him until he snatched her up and kissed her senseless.

Now it was her turn to sigh. Mariah took her mild

awareness of his maleness as a healthy sign in herself and a great sign for being able to find him someone.

Elliston slid the tablet back across the desk. "They're all my age or younger. They're like the women on all the dating sites. And I'm sure they're all very nice."

"They are," Mariah agreed. "I make sure of that."

Elliston nodded. "I guess I was hoping to find a little more maturity in my potential matches."

Mariah laughed before she could stop herself. She covered her mouth with her hand, but his narrowing gaze said she'd been caught indulging. The last thing she needed was to alienate a client with her oddball sense of humor. She was messing up as badly with Elliston as she had with his alleged uncle, John Monroe.

She tamed her smile and cleared her throat. "Am I to understand that you want me to find you someone who is older than you are?" Mariah asked to confirm.

Elliston nodded. "Yes. I think I do want that." He waved a hand at the tablet. "I've dated them already. They want a house, babies, and they get aggressive when they find out I have enough money to give that to them immediately. My perfect date is not that kind of woman. Mine is someone who just wants dinner and the pleasure of my company. That's harder to find than you might think. That's why I came to you."

Mariah nodded. "No, no. I quite believe you. However…" she paused for effect, "you need to know that mature women want things just as passionately as younger women. They just want different things than a house and babies. They want things like serious attention and utmost respect. How long is your attention span, Elliston? An older woman will demand you give her a lot of it. At the risk of being too blunt, that includes any time spent in bed."

Elliston favored her with his grin again. It really was one of his most appealing qualities. Mariah couldn't help but return it.

"I'm a great team player. I'm sure she and I can design a relationship that suits us both. The bed stuff is down the line anyway. Bed partners, like beautiful women, are easy to come by. Finding someone worth talking to is the bigger challenge."

Mariah chuckled softly. "Okay then. You've convinced me your request is sincere. Give me a couple of days to comb my database again. What's your *maturity* ceiling on age?"

He shrugged one shoulder. "I don't know. I'm pretty open-minded. What's the oldest woman in your database?"

Laughter again slipped right out of her mouth. If she wasn't so jaded, she might consider putting herself on Elliston's list. He was so… what was the word she searched for… *refreshing*? Yes, his attitude was refreshing.

"My oldest client is sixty-five and would not be a good match for you. She's a racing engineer who likes to go bungee jumping and zip lining through forests. She hates to read and watch TV. You two would never work. There would be no quiet dinners and pleasant conversations."

Elliston's answering laughter had that masculine grin permanently attaching itself to his face. "I don't know…" he teased.

Mariah shook her head. "I'll keep my recommendations for you to women under forty-five. That two decade mark is a hard dividing line. Even one decade can be a serious challenge."

"Challenge I can handle," Elliston said. "Being bored to death is my problem."

"No one I match you with will be boring," Mariah promised.

Elliston nodded. "How fast…" he paused and looked guilty. "I know this isn't like just drawing a random numbered person out of your data. But the fundraising gala is two weeks from now and…" he waved to the tablet. "I really don't want to have to take one of them. The place will be swarming with eligible bachelors from the tri-state. I'd like the woman I'm with to at least look like she's paying attention to me."

Insecurity, Mariah thought, as she nodded. It was something everyone struggled with until they met that one person who saw only them.

Now it was her turn to sigh. Maybe she wasn't as jaded as she thought.

"I'm going to work on this today and tomorrow. Hopefully, I'll have some more choices for you by Friday."

"I don't mind any extra costs you have for the re-do. I just didn't know how to say what I wanted before. I should have been more open from the start," Elliston said.

"Yes. Open is good. I highly appreciate a man with an open mind and an open wallet," Mariah joked. "So let me get back to this and I'll get back to you as soon as I have some options."

CHAPTER THREE

"Here. I made you some hot tea with chamomile. It won't iron out those worry lines crossing your barely forty year old face, but it might settle down those jingling nerves of yours. You're muttering to yourself again, Mariah. I heard you all the way in the kitchen."

She lifted the mug from the serving tray and sipped. No dainty cups in her mother's household. "Thanks, Mom."

"You're welcome. Now when are you moving out? Someone as successful as you are shouldn't be consigned to living in this tiny patio home with me. I know Dan left you enough cash to buy another place. I mean... you're welcome to stay, but staying with me just makes it look like that selfish prick financially took you off at the knees."

Mariah snorted at the blunt comments and at her mother's swearing. People often thought she'd gotten her bluntness from her Air Force Colonel father. That could have been the case, but it wasn't. She'd gotten it from

Georgia Bates, silver-haired smart-ass extraordinaire, and possibly the best mother on the planet.

"Andrew's getting ready to take the bar next year. Did you ever tell him what his bastard of a father did—or at least tried to do—to you?" Georgia asked.

"No," Mariah said, shaking her head. "And I don't intend to. I didn't tell Amanda either. With the baby coming, she doesn't need the stress. Randy's promotion came through. They're already having to move from Long Beach to Norfolk. Amanda is full up on things to worry about. The divorce was hard enough on her. She cries every time it comes up."

Georgia sniffed. "That's baby hormones. I know you raised her to be smarter about men. In my opinion, Dan's completely redefining what being an ass means. Criminal charges. I can't believe he did that to the mother of his children. What's really criminal is that twenty-something blonde he's boffing these days."

"Mom, please… just let it go. God knows I have. The kids don't need to be part of Dan's divorce vendetta against me. For better or worse, he's still their father."

"It's been *for worse* since you left your marriage and that's all on him. I swear that's all I'm going to say about the matter. I'm just mad. Your heart wasn't the only one he broke, Mariah. You married him so young that Dan felt like my own son. But if he'd really been my child, I would have done a lot better job raising him. I'm almost glad Ted died before this happened. He'd have gone for Dan's balls."

Her mother's words instantly made her think of John's description of what her rant did to him. Maybe she'd been channeling her father. Mariah relaxed only when her mother patted her shoulder. Her father had died of a heart attack when she was a freshman in college. Her mother had grieved terribly for all the years it took her to get her PhD. Then one day her mother started living again. She'd been a terrific grandmother. She'd soon be a great-grandmother in every sense of that term. Not bad for a sharp, healthy woman in her early sixties who could out swear most men when she got angry.

"Bill was great. He practically handled it all for me. Everything got dismissed and no records will be kept of the charges. But I promise you that Dan is the least of my problems at the moment. I have a couple of serious decisions to make, one of which has me stumped."

Georgia grunted. "Why? What's up? Is it anything you can discuss?"

Mariah laughed wryly. "It's no big secret, I guess. More and more young men are starting to ask for an older woman to date. This is not because they think older women are sexy or fun though. It's because they don't want to date a younger woman who wants the whole relationship package. They act like it's wrong for a woman of childbearing age to want marriage and babies. What is wrong with men these days?'

"Not a damn thing," Georgia said. "Women are the ones who've changed. A woman doesn't want to do the real work of shopping for the right guy any more. She picks one from one of those dating sites and then expects him to instantly step up to meet her relationship goals. What about genuine chemistry? What about taking the time to smile across the dinner table? It takes time and persistence, and maybe ten pounds of luck to find the right person.

Men need time to figure things out way more than women do. Love, marriage, and family should not be a goal anyway. It's a special gift, not something to barter."

"Yes, Mom." Mariah answered simply because any complex answer would have extended the rant. "Got any friends near my age looking for the perfect man to date? Looks like I suddenly have openings for older women. Maybe I can offer them a discount to be listed."

Georgia thought for a moment. "I might. Let me think about it. How about you list them for free and let the guy pick up the tab for it. In my day, men paid their way into a woman's heart."

"I'll see if my budget can afford it," Mariah promised.

When her mother left the room, she quietly sighed in relief and went back to looking for Elliston's perfect woman.

CHAPTER FOUR

THE ONLY HALF-SUITABLE WOMAN IN HER DATABASE turned out to be forty-three, which was just over the decade mark she'd set for herself in her search. It didn't surprise her that Elliston approved Lynn's appearance and bio, even though the woman visibly looked older than him. They'd even met for coffee once. From that, they'd cemented tonight's date—a date where Mariah hovered in the background like a spying mother.

Good thing she had a legitimate reason to be there, at least as legitimate as every other person attending, because she too was a contributor. But this was not how the perfect dates she arranged were supposed to work. For one thing, she was not supposed to get directly involved. Or spy on them just because she was a tad concerned.

Either the chemistry was there for the couple or it wasn't. Her clients paid a considerable amount for her to do their searching. She charged a price to be listed and a price to be matched. Someone could pay the matching

price or just hope Mariah eventually picked them. Males—
true to their biological urges and their earning potential—
seemed to order the matching more often since it was
double the price of just being listed in the database.

However, there was one universal she'd seen in the year
she'd been in business. Most clients wanted dates who were
younger than them, or at least they wanted someone no
more than their age, which was the root of her problem
now. It wasn't what Elliston McElroy had asked for and
she'd had a tough time sincerely believing someone his age
wanted to spend time with someone so much older.

Did those May men and December women sometimes
work out? Sure, they did—out in the predatory wild of
bars, singles groups, and online hookup apps. Sometimes
those relationships did beat the odds against them and
lasted. They just weren't something she wanted to base her
business model on.

"Now I understand why my instincts told me to run
like hell the other day. Do you always spy on your clients?"

Mariah closed her eyes briefly. What did it say about
her that she still recognized his voice after two weeks had
gone by. It said she'd been celibate too long. That's what it
said.

Her divorce had been final for nearly a year, but Dan
hadn't touched her for almost a year before that. He'd
moved into another bedroom the moment she'd turned in
her radio show resignation. She still made money off the
syndication of the show, but what she was doing was
helping her find her soul again.

"Detective Monroe."

"John," he corrected.

Mariah's mouth twisted into a reluctant smile. "Okay. How are you doing, *John*?"

He looked off at his nephew. "Did you really fix him up with someone old enough to be his mother?"

Something that had been blooming inside her suddenly wilted to dust. Had she really been nursing some fantasy about this man? Mariah looked across the room to Elliston and nodded her chin. "Elliston is such a nice man. Are you really his uncle?"

John turned to face her. "You didn't answer my question."

Mariah shrugged. "You didn't answer mine."

"Uncle John... you came."

John bent to offer his shorter nephew a man hug. He smirked as he met her gaze.

"Satisfied now?" he asked.

Mariah laughed. "Not really."

Elliston looked between them, a grin lighting his face. "You two know each other?"

"Not really," Mariah said again, enjoying the irritation lighting John's gaze. "We met as part of an ongoing investigation. Your uncle was so charming, I've decided not to hold the investigation against him. We were just making nice with each other when you walked over."

She raised a brow when John opened his mouth to deny her story, but it only took him two seconds to realize he'd have to confess the truth... or come up with a better lie.

"Touché," he said.

It was the oddest thing, but she just couldn't stop herself from laughing. Elliston and his uncle apparently

23

brought out the wicked in her. She turned a bright smile towards her two clients. "I think everyone in Cincinnati and Northern Kentucky turned out for this. Let's hope they all made a large contribution."

Elliston nodded. "I knew the app I created for the fundraiser was going to get some traction, but I underestimated their interest in seeing my other work. I almost can't believe this. I should have at least put more business cards in my pockets."

Mariah dug in her purse and pulled out the three she'd taken from him the first time he'd come to see her. She carried them around because she'd liked him so much. "Here. You can replace them later. Don't miss any opportunities."

Snorting, John dug in his jacket before pulling out his wallet. He dug out three cards as well and handed them over to a now chuckling Elliston.

"Gee, thanks. Why couldn't you two be my parents? Mom and Dad didn't have any on them tonight," he said before turning to his date.

Elliston's tasteless joke deserved an eye roll from his date, but he seemed to be unaware that she was nearer her and John Monroe's age than his. Mariah winced a little at the pressure they'd all accidentally put on the woman. Lynn Carson, an entrepreneur herself, merely smiled. She seemed unconcerned about any of it and pulled her phone out of a teeny, tiny sparkly gold shoulder purse resting against one curvy hip. She pulled Elliston's hand up, put one of his business cards in his palm, then took a picture of it.

Lynn smiled genuinely at him when he beamed at her. "There. Now you have something electronic to forward...

and you can get them to give you their phone number this way. It's a twofer."

Mariah breathed out when Elliston turned that grin she found so appealing in her direction. "Thank you, Mariah. Tonight has truly been perfect," he said.

Mariah nodded—message received. Then Elliston and Lynn wandered off, leaving her alone again with John.

"How old is she?" John asked sharply. "You look younger than she does."

Mariah looked at him and made a zipper sign across her lips.

"Are you ever going to really talk to me?" he demanded.

"Sure. Just stop asking me questions about my clients. If you want to know more details about her, ask your nephew."

John grunted. "Yeah… okay. I get that."

"Good," Mariah said. "Now that I've seen what I came to see, I believe I'll be leaving. Can't say it was a pleasure to see you again, but it was just as interesting as the first time."

John stopped her with a hand on her arm. "Have coffee with me."

"Coffee? It's eight o'clock at night. My mother yells at me if I pace the house and keep her awake."

"You live with your mother?" John asked.

"I do now," Mariah said. "My ex got the house."

"How the hell did that happen?"

Mariah shrugged. "Something about him working to put me through college and how he was the primary reason I'd gotten wealthy, instead of it being my hard work like I'd believed. When calculated through divorce math, it apparently added up to an amount very similar to my half of our house."

"That's bullshit."

"That's divorce," Mariah corrected. "I'm going to buy another house. It's going to be a while though, unless my mother throws me out. I cramp her style. She's a party hound."

John's reluctant laughter over her comments made her chest warm with delight. There was nothing better to her than a man with a good sense of humor. But the rest of the package? Being a detective. Being a demanding nosy ass. God, it was like she was a magnet for men like Dan and him.

She caught him looking at Elliston, who put his hand on Lynn's arm to get her attention. He stayed attached to her while he listened to what she had to say in reply to his question.

And so it begins... Mariah reluctantly shook off her happier musings. "I could stand here and watch them all night, but only because they're having a good time together. Just so you can get your report straight, I don't normally chaperone."

"Now that sounded genuine," John said.

Mariah considered it for a moment. "It was. I like your nephew."

"So you do believe me."

Mariah laughed. "No. I believe Elliston. He's the one who cried uncle when he saw you."

John sighed. "Is it because of what I do for a living?"

"Is what?"

"You know what," John accused. "You putting me off."

"Off what?" Mariah asked.

"Liking you," John ground out. "Stop playing games. I know you can tell I'm interested."

"I don't date clients."

"But I'm not a client," John reminded her.

"I draw a different line," Mariah said carefully.

"Erase it," John ordered.

"And I just got divorced."

"From someone that took your house from you. Are you still pining?"

Mariah huffed. "No, I'm not pining. I'm just not interested. I'm… off men for a while… a good long while."

"How long?" John asked.

"Why are you pressing me so hard?" she asked, finding rationality in the blunt question.

"Because you're the most plain speaking woman I've ever met and I can see that extends to anyone you care about. Your ex is an idiot."

"My ex is Senior Detective Daniel Luray."

John wiped a hand over his eyes and said a pithy word or two under his breath.

"I take it you know him," Mariah observed, fascinated when John turned crimson again.

He finally nodded. "Yes. I'm working with him on a project."

Mariah shrugged. "Doesn't surprise me. At his level, nearly everyone interacts with Dan sooner or later. I'm sure he's already shared his suspicions about my business with you."

"Like most divorced men, Dan complains a lot," John said.

"Neither denying nor admitting," Mariah observed. "I feel a shift has taken place between us. I've morphed into a two headed Hydra right before your eyes."

"No," John denied. "That's not it."

"Bet it kicked that coffee idea to the curb though, didn't it?"

Reluctantly, John nodded. "It would make my work with him harder."

"Again… no surprise here," Mariah said.

"My project with him isn't going to last forever."

Mariah sighed and bowed her head. She lifted it only after several moments of debate about how honest to be.

"John, if I were a different female, I'd turn that coffee date into a Bourbon one, and then I'd seduce you. Not for your sake, but for mine. One—because I hate being celibate. Two—for the pleasure of knowing Dan was working alongside my new lover. Divorced women can be petty and vindictive, especially when they have an ex like I have. However, I'm not even going there in fantasy. Do you want to know why?"

"I'm riveted. Why?" John demanded.

"Because I like you as much as I like your nephew. And no one deserves to be treated badly. Watch your back, John. Dan is not the ethical straight-shooter he once was. I don't know what changed him, but something has. By the time we split, the once great father and husband was completely gone."

Needing to shut herself up, Mariah turned and walked away before she ended up answering that needy look John had given her when she'd confessed to liking him.

CHAPTER FIVE

Georgia motioned to the dining table. "Okay, ladies. Food's all ready. Let's eat before Mariah gets home."

The women laughed as they filed down both sides of the table filling plates.

"I don't know if I can. I'm too nervous to eat. I can't believe I actually came here."

Reaching out, Georgia took her younger friend's arm and guided her to the table. On her best day, Jellica was forty going on twenty. It astounded her how few women had any real confidence in themselves. "You're going to be just fine. Eat now. It'll only be worse if you wait."

Georgia patted the woman's shoulder before pushing on it gently. It was always hard for her to deal with women friends who were afraid to make decisions, especially simple ones like eating.

"Why am I here, Georgia? I'm too old for this and the whole dating thing at our age is just ridiculous. I can't believe you talked me into this idiocy."

Georgia snickered as her head turned. "Quit complaining, Trudy. You're getting free food you didn't have to cook yourself for once. Enjoy it while you can."

Chef Trudy Baxter frowned as she peered down at the buffet of nearly unidentifiable potluck dishes. "I like only cooking for myself."

"You do not," Georgia argued. "I eat with you at least three times a week."

"Only because I cook better than you do," Trudy argued.

"You're a famous chef, you eyelash batting idiot."

"Idiot—I love that. You're always so kind. And I *was* a famous chef, once upon a time," Trudy corrected, frowning. "Now I'm just a retired restaurant owner with far too much free time on her hands obviously."

"Stop bad-mouthing yourself. You cook for friends and charities." Georgia snorted and shook her head. "Why am I wasting my breath arguing? Get a damn plate, Trudy. You're just here to keep Mariah from killing me. I was supposed to make her a list, not throw a potluck party. I got carried away."

"That must be a rare treat for a plodding harlot like you," Trudy answered, grinning. She looked at something yellow and then back to Georgia. "What did I tell you about using those recipes on the back of the corn can?"

"Will you just freaking eat," Georgia ordered sharply, pointing at the food.

Rolling her eyes, Trudy picked up a plate. "I can only imagine what your sex life must have been like with your husband. Was Ted into being bossed around?"

"Yes. We took turns at it," Georgia spat at her

tormentor. She reached out, scooped up a helping of corn casserole, and plopped it onto Trudy's plate. "And yes, I made it from the recipe on the can. It's got fake cheese in it too."

Trudy glared at the offending glop of yellow nuggets. "Gross."

"So are your comments, you celibate sow."

Trudy's laugh over the insult happened just before the front door opened. Georgia winced and wiped her hands on her slacks. "She's early. Shit..."

"...is about to hit the proverbial Mariah fan," Trudy finished, putting her grinning attention on other dishes. "Do you really expect me to eat food I can't identify?"

Rolling her eyes, Georgia headed to talk to her daughter.

"MOM..." MARIAH SAID WEARILY, SINKING DOWN ON the guest room bed as she tried to take it in. She eyed the closed bedroom door, wishing she'd never come home tonight. "How many women did you invite?"

"Twenty-seven because I was sure some wouldn't show up."

Mariah rubbed her forehead. "Okay. So how many are actually here?"

"Thirty four or so. Word got around. No, make that thirty-three. Trudy doesn't count. She's not interested, but frankly, the woman needs to get laid. It's been like a decade for her."

Mariah's hand fell away. Her shock was now complete.

What kind of business did her mother think she was running? She made it sound as bad as Dan did. "I'm not running a service to get women laid."

Georgia waved her hand. "You're so sensitive. That's not what I meant, Mariah."

"Well, what exactly did you mean?" Mariah demanded, irritation making her tone sharp.

She rose not waiting for an answer to her question. Logically, she knew her mother had been trying to help, but now what was she supposed to do with all those needy, and desperate, women? Client acceptance was a rigorous process for her. This was all her fault for telling her fix-it mother about a shortage she wasn't even sure she wanted to fill.

Mariah groaned softly as her gaze took in the claustrophobic dimensions of the small bedroom. She really needed to find her own place where she could vent to the walls instead of to a woman who couldn't stop herself from over-fixing everything around her.

"I never realized how many unattached females I knew over the age of forty until you asked that question. Look at the bright side, at least there's food," Georgia offered as a penance. "Everyone who came brought a potluck dish. Some of it's even good enough to eat."

Mariah laughed only because angry swearing was a habit she could have all too easily picked up living under a roof again with Georgia Bates, military wife. She raised a hand instead, giving in ungracefully, because what else could she do? The women were here already.

"Fine. I'll be out there in ten minutes. But just know

that I may not accept any of them. I'm not promising anyone anything."

Georgia shrugged. "Fine. I never promised them anything either."

"Good," Mariah said. "Because my male clients, even though some do want to date older women, have certain criteria for their matches. They expect successful, educated partners—not lonely housewives looking for boredom relief."

Georgia fisted her hands on her hips. "I think what they want is the same thing every man wants. They're just playing your expensive game to get you to do their hard work for them. Seems a little bit lazy to me, but I guess those twenty plus weddings prove you're doing something right."

"Mother…" Mariah warned, using the formality she knew her mother hated.

"Stop worrying. I knew better than to raise their hopes."

"Mother…" Mariah said softer. "This is not the way things are done."

"Well, it's a good thing then that we'll at least get food out of it. I put everyone in the Florida room so you could look at them in the daylight. Not a speck of foundation on any that I could tell so all the lines and wrinkles ought to be obvious. It shouldn't be hard to judge which ones will make a good enough high class showing."

"Mother…" Mariah said again, this time too exasperated to be stern.

"Don't forget to grab a plate on your way," Georgia ordered, opening the bedroom door and sliding out of it.

IT SURPRISED BOTH HER AND HER MOTHER WHEN Mariah actually came up with a list of eight potential women from the potluck attendees. They chatted about the women as they put plastic wrap over all the food worth keeping.

"Trudy's on my list. She's actually more like my typical female client. Maybe she's not into real dating at the moment, but I bet she wouldn't mind a few outings just for fun. Some of my clients just want an occasional companion with poise. Tell me more about Ann Lynx, though. She looks great for her age and didn't reek of desperation."

Georgia stopped wrapping to think. "Ann's a long-time widow. Her nest is truly empty now that her son's getting married. I know I told you about her. Her daughter got busted up serving in the Marines. Girl came home and ended up marrying her childhood sweetheart. She was gone for over eight years. I'm surprised Nicholas North never came to see you."

"Nicholas North? Wow. He's from old money," Mariah said.

Georgia nodded. "Georgia says he's a very good man who loves her daughter madly. That's better than money."

Mariah shrugged. "Dan and I certainly didn't marry for money. We were both in school."

"No, you didn't, but I sometimes wonder now about Dan's motives. You gave him a cushy lifestyle he would never have achieved on his own."

Mariah huffed. "We didn't break up over money. And people fall out of love all the time."

"And some—like you—get pushed out of it," Georgia replied.

Mariah rolled her eyes, definitely not wanting to cover that ground again, even if she did still sometimes wonder what happened to her former relationship. Everything was great until one day it simply wasn't anymore.

"Back to the women who came tonight. Do you think Ann is really interested in finding someone new?"

"Honestly? No," Georgia said.

Mariah laughed. Her mother was blunt to the point of conversational pain. "Why do you say that? You told me everyone who came here was interested."

Georgia turned and dug some plastic containers out of a nearby cabinet. "Oh, Ann's interested, but not necessarily in anything real. She came because Trudy and I made her. Ann's a happy widow, but her children are pressuring her to date. I think you represent a way she can make enough of a show of fake dating to keep her children off her back. All she has to do is tell them she's using a service."

Mariah frowned as she considered that info. Ann's lack of interest wouldn't work well with a male client wanting a real relationship. Usually she had the opposite problem with people wanting more than she could or anyone else could deliver.

"Do you feel like I ever pressure you to date?" Mariah asked, relieved when her mother laughed.

"No, and I would never let you," she said firmly. "Not all mother-child relationships are as honest as ours though."

Mariah nodded as she wrapped the last dish. "Children just want their parents to be happy."

Georgia nodded. "Happiness doesn't always have to

involve marriage and a man. Happy at my age can mean a lot of things. Ann's only in her early 50s. I can't speak for women her age. I lost your father then."

Mariah stopped and looked at her mother. "Do you still miss him?"

Georgia stopped spooning leftovers to think about it. "Not as much as I used to. He was a royal pain to live with after he retired. I do miss the sex, though. It was the glue that made the rough patches worth it between us. I always, always looked forward to that man coming home to me."

Mariah laughed and hung her head. She groaned a little. "Glad to hear Dad was a stud."

"Are you not dating because I'm not?" Georgia asked, the thought just occurring to her.

Mariah's head came flying up. "Of course not," she denied. "Because of Dan, I hate men right now. This is not a good attitude to have when you want to date. I'm hoping it's a phase that will pass. I miss the sex too."

"Physician, heal thyself..." Georgia quoted.

Mariah snorted over the quote. "Except I'm not a physician. Nor apparently was I an expert at choosing a life partner either. My life has gotten very ironic given what I'm trying to do for a living."

Georgia fisted a hand on her hip. "Don't let Daniel Luray become your standard for men. If I ever found a man I thought would be as good in bed as your father, I'd at least give him a go to see if I was right. The only reason that's likely never going to happen is that I'm not looking."

"You could start," Mariah said to stop the lecture. But it didn't work.

Georgia lifted a shoulder and let it fall. "I know. It's

NEVER IS A VERY LONG TIME

both my fault and my decision. And it doesn't mean there aren't any good men out there. You know it's all relative, Mariah. We've talked about this before. A woman can decide to be divorced and bitter, or she can decide to open up again. Either way will be no one's call but hers. I know Dan had his own bedroom well over a year before the actual divorce. You're way too young to go without sex for so long."

Mariah chuckled and gave her mother a real smile. "I have a doctorate and am still only half as smart as you. How did you get that way? Tell me the truth."

"I said your father was good in bed," Georgia admitted. "I didn't say he was easy to live with outside of it. Military men are a lifelong education money can't buy. I was secretly glad when you married a civilian, or at least I was until Dan turned into a greedy bastard."

"You never told me that before… I mean, about being glad I didn't marry someone in the military."

Georgia shrugged. "I was happy my grandchildren wouldn't be moving every three years. Ted and I had a good life, and we did the best by you kids as we could, but it wasn't always easy. Based on how exhausted I was by the time you hit college, I decided being settled in one place for most of your life was a better way to live."

"Yet you didn't blink when Amanda married Randy."

"They were high school sweethearts. That's a whole different matter. She loved him and he loved her. You didn't blink either."

Mariah sighed. "For the same reasons. Because she loved him… and yes, I could see he really loved her. I was only worried because I didn't want my divorce to affect

37

their belief that love was worth…" She stopped and looked at her very smart mother. "Love. That's why it works or doesn't. When I married Dan, we worked because we loved each other then."

Georgia lifted her hands.

Mariah walked around the bar and hugged her mother. "I'll try to remember to let love in again if it shows up a second time in my life. Will you?"

She laughed when her mother's only answer was a long, exasperated sigh.

CHAPTER SIX

DELLA'S KNOCK HAD HER HEAD LIFTING. SHE ALWAYS appreciated that her assistant knew not to jar her out of her work. She tended to get lost in whatever task held her attention. The woman's deep in-drawn breath followed by a resigned sigh had her sitting straighter in her chair though.

"What is it, Della?"

"John Monroe is back to see you."

Mariah wilted with relief. Then her pulse sped up. How could she be excited to see him? Especially after he admitted he was working with Dan.

"It's okay," Mariah said finally. "He really is Elliston McElroy's uncle. We can take Detective Monroe on as a client if he's truly interested."

Della frowned and shook her head. "Your ex is here with him."

Mariah put a hand on her forehead and leaned an elbow on her desk. Just for a moment she allowed herself a mini-meltdown, but needed to get hold of herself before she screamed.

"Alright," Mariah said finally, proud of herself for her calm answer.

"Your ex said he and Mr. Monroe are here to serve you with a subpoena."

"Not alright then."

"No, Dr. Bates. It's not alright. What do you want me to do with them?"

"Unless you brought a gun with you to work… nothing. I'll just have to deal with them the old fashioned way."

Mariah stood and braced herself on the desk with both hands. She slipped her feet back into the low, black, dressy heels she'd thrown on that morning instead of looking for more comfortable shoes.

Her closet at her former house had been bigger than her entire bedroom at her mother's. She really was going to have to get her own place soon. She'd kicked the uncomfortable things under her desk while she worked, but a business woman couldn't accept legal service for court in bare feet, could she?

She pulled her jacket off the back of her chair and tugged it on as well. Standing straight and now fully dressed again, Mariah walked around the desk only to pause in the doorway. "Stay close, Della. If my secret Kung Fu powers kick in like I hope, I'm going to need help burying the bodies later."

Della's low laughter over her joking eased her trepidation a fraction, but it was all the humor she could reach for in that awful moment.

In her client waiting area, the first person she saw was Detective John Monroe, who stood glaring at her smugly grinning ex-husband. She spared him a look first before glaring at Dan herself.

"Don't you have real criminals you should be chasing? What is it now, Dan?"

He held out a legal sized sealed envelope to her. "The prosecutor's office has a witness who says you paid her to sleep with a client. This subpoena is for your financial records, Mariah. They want to have a look at your books."

"They do… or *you* do?" Mariah asked, taking the envelope from him. "I'll see Bill gets these. He'll advise me what to do. Is that all, Dan?"

"Nothing Bill does is going to change this, Mariah. You have no choice except to show us your dirty money."

She glanced over at John Monroe to see how he was reacting to Dan's callousness. The man looked nearly ready to explode. John Monroe's face was flushed in anger and the fierce glare aimed at her ex could have leveled a building. Strangely, Dan seemed impervious to the other man's growing upset. She let her gaze linger on John Monroe's wide shoulders as she answered because she couldn't seem to make him meet her eyes.

"Dan, people always have choices. You just keep making bad ones."

"So do you," Dan replied.

Mariah shrugged. "There's where we disagree. Now if you'll both excuse me, I'm expecting a client shortly." It was a lie, but she felt no guilt for it, none at all. She wanted both men gone before she privately looked at the latest legal torment.

"It's only a matter of time until I shut you down, Mariah."

She lifted her chin and glared into the face of the father of her children. Remembering that always helped her tolerate the snake when his venom started spewing in her direction.

But when... when had Dan become the heartless man in front of her? What had happened to that laughing, sexy boy she'd met in college? And as usual, that pondering affected her mouth.

"I don't understand any of this, Dan. You got the house and enough money to care for it for at least twenty years. As a senior detective, you make a good salary with your work. Why are you so determined to see me financially ruined? Are you really that mad at me just for changing jobs?"

Dan gave her an evil look, but she'd seen that meanness so often now, she'd become numb to it.

"Your old job calls you every month, Dr. Bates. We both know they'd take you back in a heartbeat. You should go back to your real work while you still can. This farce has already cost you our marriage. Do you want it to take the rest of your life down too? Your reputation used to mean everything to you."

Mariah shook her head and looked away. She was never, never going to understand Dan's determination to ruin her. It wasn't like splitting up had even been her idea. He was the one who'd moved out of her bed and then eventually left the house all together. He'd been the one who originally filed for the divorce.

But now... now she was just glad he'd ended it. She'd

have never found her calm center living in the same house with him while he acted this way. There had been no peace between them since Dan got the house, but at least there had been distance.

"If you're done torturing me for today, I'd really like you to just go," she said softly, her emotional weariness showing up at last in her plea.

She knew when Dan finally softened because he said her name softly in return and stepped towards her. Mariah stepped determinedly back and held the legal envelope out between the two of them.

"You're delusional if you think for one minute I'd let you ever comfort me again. Those days are over for good. You've served this legal crap and I've accepted receipt of it. Now I need you to leave—both of you. I'm done being polite."

John cleared his throat. "Let's go, Luray… before you cross any more lines."

Dan's concerned gaze changed to irritation as it swung from her to Detective John Monroe. "You're a real stickler for rules, aren't you, John?"

"You have no idea how true that statement is," John answered him back.

Mariah realized it was the first time John had spoken since they'd arrived. He looked ready to drag Dan out of her office, and given his greater size, could probably do it if he wanted. But what was his role in Dan's grand scheme to destroy her? Mariah couldn't figure John out any more than she could Dan.

John turned and opened her office door, glaring at Dan until he finally walked through it ahead of him. He turned

back to look at her—a strange penetrating gaze to be sure
—then followed Dan out.

And that was the third time in a week she'd seen the
man. Was it too much to hope it would be the last?

When she and Della were alone again, Della bit her lip.
Mariah chuckled despite her stress. "I know. We don't really
have a client coming in. I lied."

Della instantly wilted in relief. "Great. I thought I'd
screwed up."

Mariah chuckled. "You didn't." She held up the
envelope, all the while trying hard not to stare at it. "Guess
I'm calling Bill again. I can't imagine who Dan got to lie to
the prosecutor's office. I also can't imagine why he'd go to
all that trouble."

"You could always seduce John Monroe. He'd probably
tell you just to spite your ex. There were a couple of
moments where I thought he was going to yank him out of
here. You didn't see it, but when Dan took that step toward
you, John went all tense and made fists. That's a sure tell.
He wasn't going to let your ex get his hands on you."

Mariah shook her head. "Dr. Livingston, no amount of
higher education can ever adequately explain the
motivations of men. I don't know why Dan is out to get
me. I don't know what role John Monroe is playing.
Frankly, I don't know anything."

Della grunted. "Well, I know something."

Mariah tilted her head to listen. "What's that?"

"John Monroe wants to protect you. Everything about
his body fairly screamed it the whole time he was here.
Whatever his role is, I think he's secretly on your side. I also
don't think your ex knows it."

Holding yet another legal problem in her hands, Mariah laughed at the incredible optimism of her young assistant. "That's a great theory, but my days of believing in white knights are long gone. Well, except for one and I need to go call him now. Bill isn't going to believe this."

CHAPTER SEVEN

"HER NAME IS BETH STANLEY. IS SHE A CLIENT?" BILL asked.

Mariah couldn't have been more shocked if Bill had slapped her. "Yes. She is. Beth Stanley brought the charge against me?"

Bill nodded. "That's what it says, but Ms. Stanley wasn't willing to say much about the matter. Given the charges, I find that strange. It makes their case weak."

"She paid to be listed in the database but never went on any dates. Her criteria was too specific for me to match her easily."

"Explain that statement to me," Bill commanded.

"Beth Stanley was only willing to date men above a certain income level, preferably those who didn't have to work for a living. She said she wanted to have a companion and be entertained, not be some man's slave."

"Sounds like a lovely woman," Bill said dryly.

Mariah shrugged. "Some people know exactly what

they want. Others are open-minded. I don't judge a person by their ability to know what they need, but why would she lie about this, Bill? She came in, paid the fee, made her video, and then left. I have sixty other women who did the same. Why would Beth Stanley plot with Dan to ruin me?"

"I don't know. At this point, it's just her word against yours, which won't take her far unless she names the man she allegedly serviced. However, you're probably going to have to provide the prosecutor's office with your financials, and perhaps even name some clients. I unfortunately don't see you getting out of all of this. We could ask them to review the records discreetly, but it would be up to the judge whether or not they honor our request to keep them private. If they get entered into court records, they won't be kept that way."

Mariah groaned loudly and rose to pace. "*Why in the world is he doing this to me?* He wants me to go back to my old job. What would Dan have to gain by that?"

"I don't know, Mariah."

"What happens if I refuse to turn over my records?"

"You would look like you're hiding something." Bill pushed the subpoena to the side. "I suggest giving them last year's profit and loss statement, but not client names. Let's start with that. It will at least buy you a bit more time to think about all this."

Mariah nodded. "Alright. Let's do that." She came back to the chair and lifted her purse from it. "I'm going to dinner. I need Chinese food. And a fortune cookie with some positive news in it."

"Want some company?"

Mariah shook her head. "Thanks, but no. I need some time alone."

Bill nodded. "I'm sorry I don't have better news, Mariah."

Mariah smiled sadly. "I'm sorry I don't have a nicer ex-husband. The divorce was hard, but this is the stuff of nightmares. I was a good wife and a good mother. I did love him once, but even the memories of that love are nearly gone now. Something's happened to Dan. I don't know what, but he's not the man I married. It's hard to feel anything but loathing for who he's become."

"I've often thought the same thing," Bill said softly. "He changed a lot when the kids hit high school. Dan got distant—hard-hearted even. He stopped coming over to watch ball games and wouldn't bother going for a beer with me. All he seemed to be about was his next job."

"I remember. He had to be away a lot for work back then. I used to blame his worsening moods on job stress, but now I wonder if something else was going on. We had no lack of money. We had the life everyone dreams of having. When Andrew started his last year of law school, I started my new business. Dan moved into his own room and told the kids we were fighting. Apathy from him I could understand, Bill, but he's worked to turn himself into my enemy. That's what doesn't make any sense to me."

Bill nodded. "I agree. Maybe you should hire a private investigator to dig into his private life a little."

"To investigate one of the city's most decorated detectives?" Mariah exclaimed. "No way. And besides... if there was another woman during the time we were divorcing, I think I would rather not know about her. I've handled enough disillusionment about my former marriage. That might just be the one that makes me close my business for real."

Mariah found no reasons for Dan's behavior at the bottom of her Moo-Goo-Gai-Pan, but at least her stomach was full. The two cups of plum wine she'd started with hadn't revealed anything except the need to drink a couple cups of the hot tea in front of her before she made her way home.

"Here you are. Chinese. Of course. I should have checked here first."

A shadow loomed over Mariah's table a few moments before her ex dropped into the seat across from her. Not really having anything more to say to him, Mariah lifted her teacup and sipped. Maybe she could just ignore Dan and he'd go away on his own.

"Pretending I'm not here isn't going to work," he said, reading her mind.

She lowered her teacup. "I have nothing to say to you, Dan."

"Fine. I'll say it then. I'm sorry I upset you so badly today. Seeing you hurt made me want to comfort you, Mariah. It also made me think that I was wrong to divorce you. As crazy it sounds, I think I want you back."

Mariah slid backwards into her seat. She wondered if she looked as stunned as she felt. "You're kidding."

Dan rolled his eyes. "No. I'm not kidding. Why would I kid about that?"

"You're trying to ruin me, Dan. That's not exactly a sign of true love."

Dan shook his head. "I'm not trying to ruin you, Mariah. I'm trying to save you from making the biggest mistake of your life. Don't you miss the life we had? I know I do. Give up this business, go back to the show, and let's fix this."

Mariah threw up a hand. "Dan, you somehow convinced a client of mine to lie to the prosecutor's office. That can't be fixed with an apology."

"That woman coming forward was nothing I did."

Mariah huffed. "Right—like I can ever trust what you say again. Bill's sending the paperwork to the prosecutor's office. Now get out of my sight before I call and report you for harassment."

"Mariah, don't be this way."

"What way, Dan? You mean rational? If the kids knew what you've pulled on me, they'd never speak to you again. Be grateful I'm sparing them the whole sordid truth about their father."

Dan lifted his chin and stared hard at her. "I wish there was a way to make you understand. Why did you take our perfect life away from both of us?"

Mariah lifted her tea again. "*Perfect life?* You mean, the life where my husband moved into another bedroom and stopped sleeping with me after nearly twenty years? That perfect life, Dan? You're the one who stepped away. I'm just the one who had to get used to it."

Dan leaned on the table. "I was going through a bad time. I realize now that pulling away from you was a terrible mistake." He sighed and put a hand on the table palm up. "Please think about this. I want you back, Mariah."

Mariah ignored his hand. It was remarkably easy, especially after today. "What are you hiding from me, Dan? What is this really about? Everyone that knows you suspects something strange is going on. I was just the last one to give a good damn, but all that caring got me the chance to know what it was like to be homeless."

Dan hung his head. "You know I'm going to have to sell the house in a short while. Without your steady income, I can't maintain it."

"I gave you money enough to maintain it. You don't owe a penny in mortgage. Sell it and run with what you get for all I care."

"This is not just about the house…"

"Isn't it? It's certainly not about the love, Dan. We're done with all that. We've been done a long time. Leave please before I have to make good on my threat to call you in for stalking me."

Dan stood, but leaned down close to her face. She could smell his cologne—the expensive scent was a gift she'd bought him when she'd landed the first syndicated run of her show. Now it smelled like the biggest disappointment of her life.

"I'll never believe we're over. I love you, Mariah. I always have."

Then Dan was gone.

She sipped her tea afterwards, staring at the now vacant seat again. Ten minutes later, she was gathering up her purse when she smelled a woodsy aftershave by her shoulder. Looking up for the source, she met Detective

John Monroe's apologetic gaze. "Good Lord. Will the torture of this day never end?"

"Hi. Can I sit down for a few minutes?" he asked.

"Do I really have a choice?" Mariah asked back, working not to glare.

John nodded. "Yes. But I really think you should talk to me. Despite what it might have seemed like today, I'm trying to be your friend."

"At least your threats sound more gentlemanly than Dan's," Mariah said, waving a hand to the empty chair. "I assume you watched my ex jump out of that seat and leave. You can have five minutes, *Detective*."

John slid his body into the seat, dwarfing it until the chair completely disappeared behind and under him.

"You're the biggest man I've ever seen," Mariah observed, her usual politeness filter gone.

John's instant, and very wicked, grin surprised her. "Thank you. That's exactly what every man longs to hear from the beautiful woman he's attracted to."

Mariah rolled her eyes at his compliment, but laughed at his teasing. "That's not at all what I meant." She almost sighed in girlish joy when John's smile got very wide. Such a handsome man. Too bad he was just another conniving liar.

"I know what you really meant, but it was nice to dream for a moment that one day you might actually learn just how incredibly true that statement is about me."

"And that's exactly what most men think of themselves."

"I'm not most men."

"Could have fooled me," Mariah declared. "After

serving me a subpoena based on a falsified report this afternoon, my ex just casually dropped by to ask me to come back to him. The offer was contingent on me returning to my old job, of course. I figure you got that much from what you no doubt overheard while tailing me. Now I have a question. Who are you really, John Monroe?"

John looked off. "Do you want him back?"

Mariah nearly barked out a laugh. "Dan? No. Absolutely not. I'm still grieving the loss of my marriage, but I'm learning that's very different from grieving the loss of Daniel Luray."

"Good to hear you're getting over him," John said.

"What game are you playing with me, Detective?"

John snickered. "So we're back to that. I thought we'd gotten past formalities at least."

"What game are you playing, *John*?"

He turned, met her gaze, and held it. "The kind where I keep falling for someone I shouldn't, but she's so damn charming I can't help myself. I'd like to run off with her, but that's impossible at the moment. Worse, there's no way in hell she can believe I feel this way about her. That's what kind of game."

Mariah put both elbows on the table and rested her chin in her hands. She studied his eyes, letting herself sink into the sincerity in them for a few moments. His admission certainly soothed her bruised female ego, but that didn't make him a freaking knight in shining armor. She needed to get a grip.

"You're almost as bad as him. Two cups of plum wine were not enough to hear that confession, were they?"

John shook his head. "I can't tell you anything else yet

either, but soon I will be able to. Can I ask you to trust me for a bit until I get it all sorted out?"

Mariah sighed in frustration. "Get *what* sorted out, John?"

John put one arm on the table and held her gaze again. "I'm sorting out a good woman's very complicated life."

Mariah sat up again and shouldered her purse. "Trust is a lot to ask of me right now."

"Yes. I know," John said roughly. "But a reassuring hug is out of the question at the moment."

"Too bad," Mariah said sadly. "A hug is exactly what I need."

"Mariah…"

Holding up a hand to stop him from further expressing the sympathy she'd heard when he'd said her name, Mariah slid from her seat and left Detective John Monroe, or whoever he really was, sitting there staring at her.

She honestly didn't think she could trust him and that fact made her very sad.

CHAPTER EIGHT

"If I'm being quiet, it's because I'm embarrassed. I don't even know why I'm here."

Mariah swiveled in her office chair as she considered the woman across the desk. "What bothers you most, Ann? The makeover or the dating?"

When Ann Lynx laughed and wrinkled her nose in distaste, Mariah smiled at the nervous woman. "It was a serious question."

Ann laughed again, but more softly. "I always thought there wasn't much I couldn't handle in life until I realized my children were worried about me. Every time they see me now they start hinting about me dating." Her surprised gaze roamed the office. "Even with them planting the idea in my head, using a service like *The Perfect Date* never crossed my mind. I figured such things were only for young people."

Mariah shrugged. "There are plenty of dating services that cater to mature people, though *older* doesn't exactly mean what it used to mean. I have a surprising number of younger men asking to date someone more mature. Plenty would be willing to date a good-looking woman your age."

Ann chuckled. "The young guys just want a woman to sleep with who doesn't want babies and marriage. My son is over thirty and only now wanting to settle down. David almost lost a good woman because of that kind of thinking. All Kendra wanted was a house and a couple babies. What is so wrong with that? The planet has to continue somehow."

Mariah laughed at hearing the echo of her own sentiments. "You and I are kindred souls, Ann Lynx. But my job is to keep my clients happy, not push my philosophies off on them. So if it's mature women my younger male clients want, then quality mature women are what I will give them. But for you... I have someone special in mind for you. He's not really looking for a relationship either, which is rare among those in my database. This client just needs an occasional date for a social function now and again. He uses my service for discretionary purposes. He's in his early fifties and quite handsome."

"Why isn't he married then?" Ann asked.

"He's been married several times and often to women much younger," Mariah said bluntly. "He'll tell you the same thing, so it's not like I'm giving away any secrets here. He's nearly as blunt as I am."

Ann rolled her eyes. "The day I let my children tell me who to love..." She paused then laughed. "Right... well... I guess that was a bit hypocritical of me considering here I am."

"Only a little," Mariah agreed, showing two fingers spread apart, "but vastly entertaining. For the right mature clients, I'm temporarily waiving my usual fee to be added to my database. All you have to do is agree to be in the match pool and we'll get started."

"You make it sound so easy," Ann said, slowly releasing an anxious breath.

"My part *is* pretty easy," Mariah teased. "You're the one who'll be wearing high heels and going out. I get to sit here in my office and simply feel righteous for setting the date up."

Ann giggled. "You joke around as much as your mother does."

Mariah shrugged. "But I'm always serious when I'm talking business. Are you in?"

Ann looked around once more, eyes wide. "I guess I am. Bring on the rich commitment-phobes."

"We call them perfect dates around here, and you'll be surprised how nice they are. Most just have more complicated lives than the rest of us," Mariah warned, grinning when Ann giggled again.

NOT WANTING TO FACE HER MOTHER, BECAUSE THAT meant admitting to the nosy woman that Ann Lynx was a client now, Mariah dug the yoga bag out of her truck and went to class. She hadn't gone since the divorce proceedings began.

Energized afterwards, she pulled a slouchy pink sweater over her workout clothes and decided getting a big, made-to-order salad for dinner sounded like a good idea.

She was sitting down to it when she saw John Monroe come through the door. He was wearing jeans with a Henley shirt tucked into them. The man was massive, but not overweight or anything. Just really... big.

And obviously following her.

Sighing in disgust over her pleasure to see him in something other than a suit, Mariah dug into her salad and gave herself a side order of chastisement over her foolishness.

"You sure eat alone a lot," John said casually.

Mariah shrugged. "Because the only people in my life besides my nosy mother are the two detectives who keep following me around."

"Only one of us is following you tonight. The other is preoccupied."

"With what?" Mariah asked, feigning a lack of concern. Problem was she sucked at faking anything.

"The proper question would be *with whom*, but that's all I'm able to say about the matter," John declared.

Mariah watched as John pulled out the chair across from her and sat without invitation this time. She raised an eyebrow over the action, but didn't comment when John squirmed under her gaze. Did he think she was just going to start welcoming his intrusion into her life?

"The company my ex-husband keeps is none of my business. That liberation came with the divorce, backed up by several years of endless fighting. What I'm curious about is why you keep following me."

John pursed his lips. "Like I said yesterday, I can't tell you."

Mariah rolled her eyes and then returned to eating. What else was there to do?

"Did it ever occur to you that it might be because of the exceptional way your butt looks in those tight yoga pants you're wearing? It's calling to me to rub it."

Salad nearly flew from her mouth when she laughed. She swallowed with difficulty as she got hold of herself. "Somehow I doubt that's true. God, that line wouldn't even work on a twenty year old."

John shrugged and sighed. "Fine. You looking exceptionally nice in those clothes is completely true, but you're right that it isn't why I'm keeping tabs."

Mariah huffed out an exasperated breath and pushed back from her food. "Do I need to go over your head about this, Detective Monroe? I do know your supervisor personally. Dan's acting strange, but somehow I don't think he's the one who put you on ex-wife surveillance duty. I know Dan's boss."

"Good. Don't talk to your ex. Call Chief Langley—only him. Okay?"

"You're freaking me out, Detective."

"Can't be helped, Dr. Bates."

"So we're back to that?" Mariah asked tersely.

John sighed loudly. "Unless you can quit asking questions I can't answer long enough to let me concentrate on more important things."

"Like…?" Mariah prompted.

"I told you… your exceptional body in those yoga pants. Geez, I am a guy, you know. You look fantastic. I haven't been so attracted to a woman since I was a kid. And one way or the other, I swear I'm going to find a way to kiss you and see if that's as exceptional as I think it's going to be as well."

"Oh… so you're a stalker then," Mariah declared, not missing a bite. "Wow, I haven't had one of those since I went off the air."

The glare John gave her was priceless. Her laughing over his irritation only deepened it, but verbally getting the better of him did relax her enough to go back to eating. "If you're going to sit there keeping tabs, why don't you grab some dinner while you're doing it?"

He frowned at her food. "That's not my idea of dinner."

"It's healthy, but they have great subs too," Mariah told him, unsure why she was even suggesting he eat with her.

"Don't run away," he ordered, rising to walk to the counter.

Her gaze followed his own exceptional jean-covered backside as John walked to the counter. Their mutual interest in each other's anatomies made her face heat. Was she genuinely attracted to him?

"No. You're just horny," she answered herself, digging back into her salad with more force than necessary.

Minutes later, John carried a small bowl of salad and a large sub to the table. He sat, looked at her anxiously, and then sighed heavily. Shaking his head, he unwrapped his sandwich.

"I've never once developed an interest in anyone I was assigned to protect. I don't know why it happened with you. It had to be that day in your office when you jumped to Elliston's defense. Or maybe it was at that stupid fundraiser when I saw him so pleased with that woman you set him up with. Yet you were happier than either of them. I've obviously lost my mind. The yoga butt comments alone could get me suspended."

Through his rant, one statement rang out to her. John believed he was protecting her. But from whom or from what? She'd dearly love to know. "Good to hear I can cause you problems. I'll keep that in mind if I ever get that angry about you following me around."

John rolled his eyes and took a bite of his sandwich, not answering her taunt.

Mariah smiled. He was such a normal guy, and yet... "Thanks for the yoga butt comments. Frankly, it's been a couple years since anything on my body was properly appreciated."

She burst out laughing when John choked and coughed around a bite of sandwich. Her amused reaction to his discomfort earned her yet another fierce glare and had her wondering how much she could push before he actually retaliated. The very thought of that boundary revved her sluggish engine. Whatever else came of their paths crossing, there was no doubt for her that Detective John Monroe had woke her libido from its sexual slumber.

Mariah went back to her food, finishing off the salad. She sighed into her bowl. "I'm sorry, John. I shouldn't have said that to you. It was true, but bad form to share it."

John didn't say anything. Instead, he put his hand on the table between them, palm up. It was the same thing Dan had done at the Chinese restaurant, but she couldn't seem to ignore John's hand the same way she had Dan's.

Not able to bring herself to actually take it, she did

reach out her fingertips and draw them across his very large palm. His skin was incredibly hot to her touch. She pulled her fingers back, resting only the tips of her fingers on the tips of his. They were barely touching, but it felt so... intimate.

Scarier than that though, it felt right. The rightness was out of place in their circumstances.

Swallowing hard, Mariah pulled her fingers away, only then lifting her gaze to his. "Am I in any real danger, John?"

John stared at her, narrowing his eyes as they roamed her face and hair. "Only from me embarrassing us both when I come across this table after you. I'm working to control my predator side right now. Give me a few minutes before you make any sudden moves."

Mariah giggled at the flirty threat, this time appalled at herself. Pushing her empty salad bowl aside, she leaned crossed arms on the table and stared at him.

"Our attraction to each other has no future. You know that and I know that. You work for Dan and I can't trust you. Plus, I'm never dating another police officer. I've done my civic duty, Detective. If it wasn't unethical, I'd put myself in my own database."

"I don't blame you. Some rich guy could easily give you back your rich life," John said.

Mariah shook her head and turned her gaze away from him. "My work was never about the money for me. Dan always cared about that way more than I did. And he didn't bankrupt me, he just emptied the bank temporarily. My syndication requests keep expanding. In a couple of years, it will financially be like the divorce never happened. That's why I knew I'd be okay with *The Perfect Date* even if it didn't make anything the first couple of years."

"No wonder he wants to come back," John said.

She turned back to see him still studying her. "You seem to have a poor opinion of your boss."

"I concluded Daniel Luray was an idiot the moment I met you."

"Then why are you still working for him?" Mariah asked.

"Because I have no choice… for now."

They locked gazes then, but she could read nothing in his. How she could be attracted to yet another man capable of locking her out emotionally? What deficiency in her character made her this stupid?

"Time for me to go home," Mariah said softly. "I believe I'll be dining at my mother's tomorrow night. Consider it stalker's night off."

"Mariah…" John began as she stood.

"Yes?" She waited for him to say something to stop her, even though lingering to chat with a man who refused to be truthful with her was beyond ludicrous.

"Thanks for letting me eat with you. I almost always eat alone. Elliston takes pity on me once a week and we have dinner together."

"Guess that's another reason for me to like that impressive young man," Mariah said.

John nodded. "He's a pretty decent guy for a geek."

Chuckling, she patted his shoulder—a very firm, very wide shoulder—as she passed by him. But touching him only made her want to do it more.

Now she wanted to go exploring and see if the rest of John felt that hard under her hands.

Great. This was the very reason hands off had always been her motto. She didn't touch lightly. Never had.

Touching John Monroe? Mistake. Mistake. Mistake.

CHAPTER NINE

"WHAT WORKED IN YOUR FAVOR WAS THAT BETH Stanley wasn't willing to name the client she allegedly performed the sexual favors for that were mentioned in great detail in her statement. Do you want to know what she said she did?"

Mariah gave him her best death look. "No."

Bill laughed. "I found it quite an entertaining read."

"Don't make me tell Abigail on you," Mariah warned.

Grinning, Bill went back to his notes. "They accepted the meager financials we turned over and promised to keep them discreet. I told them if we saw anything leaked to any press that we'd be suing the city of Cincinnati and all of Hamilton County for defamation and slander without cause. I also told them that particular action was nothing compared to what I intended to do if they kept insisting on seeing a full client list. I told them to get their witness to cough up a real name and we'd cough up the records on that one client. At that point, they backed way off because I was being reasonable. Their witness is obviously not willing to go that far."

"Because she's lying through her scarlet harlot teeth," Mariah said firmly.

Bill nodded. "And because I'm sure they had to advise her that perjury is very costly and can lead to jail time as well."

Mariah let out the breath she'd been holding. "So? Is *The Perfect Date* off the hook again?"

"For now," Bill said.

"Brilliant legal work." Mariah slumped down and stretched out in Bill's uncomfortable office chair so she could lean her head back. "Why am I not more relieved?"

Bill shuffled some papers, then got quiet. "I don't know, Mariah. You tell me. Did something else happen?"

Mariah pulled herself back up to a rigid seated position. "Yes. Dan tracked me down at a Chinese restaurant two nights ago and insisted he wanted me back. He said he still loves me. Can you believe he had the nerve to say that after all he's done?"

"Bullshit," Bill said, staring hard at her. "Abby and I saw him out to dinner with a woman just last night. She didn't look like the photo of your client. This woman had short, bleached-out blonde hair and was not very well done even though she was wearing designer clothes from head to toe. From my appraiser days, I can also tell you she was wearing a ruby necklace that probably cost more than the swimming pool I had installed last summer."

"I don't have the energy to care about what his relationship is to Beth Stanley or the new woman, but it doesn't surprise me that he's seeing someone. Dan made me go without sex for the last year we were still together, but I knew he wasn't doing that himself. He was too relaxed when he came home. I'm going to be mad about the sex for a good long while."

Bill chuckled. "Aren't you even a little bit heartbroken over proof Dan is moving on?"

Mariah looked away, thought about it, and then shrugged. "Maybe I should be, but I'm not. I have a bigger problem."

"How big?" Bill asked.

"Detective John Monroe big. He works with Dan—for Dan—whatever the case is. He came into the restaurant immediately after Dan left and urged me not to trust Dan. Then last night John shows up at the salad restaurant where I was having dinner alone. I don't know if the man's really protecting me like he says he is, or if he's a new kind of stalker. Strangely, he wants me to do nothing about anything Dan is doing to me. Plus, he says I should trust *him* while I wait for him to come clean at some future time he's refused to name. I don't know what to think at this point."

"Unless you're the suspect of a criminal investigation, he's in violation of your rights by not telling you why you're being followed. If you're in danger, you have a right to know. Now that you know he's tailing you, he's obligated to tell you why." Bill held up a finger and turned to his computer. "Give me two minutes to look into the guy."

For the seven minutes it actually took, Mariah waited, and felt guilty about what Bill was doing, which was stupid of her. John Monroe was obviously lying to her on a regular basis. He didn't deserve her loyalty.... did he?

"Huh," Bill muttered softly, squinting at the screen as if not believing what he was reading.

Mariah put her hand over her mouth to keep from groaning in alarm, but maybe she should use both hands and cover her ears. From the look on Bill's face, what her attorney was learning was pretty shocking.

"What?" she finally asked, bracing to hear the worst.

Bill clicked something on the keyboard, made the screen go dark, and then turned back to stare at her for a few moments. He cleared his throat like he did before delivering any bad news. Mariah groaned internally. "It's bad, isn't it?"

"I'm sorry, Mariah, but I can't tell you."

"What? You're kidding..."

"No. Telling you could jeopardize what John is doing."

What she said as she rose from the seat would have made even Georgia Bates's ears burn in embarrassment. She glared at Bill and turned to leave, stopping only when he laughed at her anger. "It's not funny, Bill."

"It is a little. Trust me that things are fine and trust Detective Monroe. Do whatever he says," Bill ordered.

She glared over her shoulder. "The man wants to take me to bed, Bill. Is that what you think I should do with him?"

Bill laughed again, looking sheepish. "Maybe you need to talk to Abby instead of me about that sort of dilemma. I'm better at the legal stuff. She handles all love crises among our friends."

"Here's what I think about your male posturing crap," Mariah declared, and lifted her middle finger to him.

"Seriously..." Bill called as she stomped out his office door. "Trust him, Mariah. He's a good man."

"Mariah?"

The dread she felt hearing her assistant say her name proved how much the stress of her life was getting to her. The slightest hesitation in Della's voice these days set her teeth on edge.

She hated Dan for making her this anxious. John Monroe was coming in a close second today though. And Bill—her "just trust him" attorney—now held third place —the traitor.

"I swear if there's a policeman of any sort in my waiting room, I'm calling my mother. She'll come and take them both out for me," Mariah said, completely out of patience.

Della's eyes widened at the threat and then she laughed. "No—no. It's not them today... it's..."

Looking over her shoulder, her grinning assistant tiptoed quietly toward her desk, stopping a couple feet from it to whisper.

"It's Dr. Colombo here to see you without an appointment and..." Della drew in a breath for the harder, but more entertaining admission. "Your mother is actually at this moment fixing our leaky toilet. I couldn't stop her, Mariah. Luckily, she was in there when Dr. Colombo arrived."

Mariah belly laughed in relief. Dr. Colombo was a handsome sweetie of a client. Her mother merely incorrigible. Compared to Bill's unwillingness to tell her the truth about John, even getting two weird problems at once didn't faze her.

"Okay, partner-in-crime. Here's what I want from you. Send the handsome Dr. Colombo in before my mother starts filling the air with curses. The toilet should keep her busy for a while, but you're to run interference if it doesn't."

Della grinned and nodded. "Yes, ma'am. I can do that. Should I ask her if she brought her gun in case the cops show up too?"

"Everyone's a comedian these days," Mariah said, smiling at her chuckling assistant's back when Della hurried back out.

"Come loose, you disintegrated piece of rubberized crap."

Georgia yelled the words, trying her best to wiggle loose the tiny water hose without breaking the tiny plastic connector pipe it was attached to.

Her face was nearly in the tank as she put both bare arms down inside for leverage as she tugged. When the hose finally gave, she got a still pressurized stream of water right in her face. Swearing, she automatically held out her hand over it to stop it which only served to send the water shooting sideways at her breasts.

"Mother effing piece of..." She was too mad to continue the oath. "Damn water shutoff," she spat, grabbing her now soaked boobs with one hand to assess the water damage to them as she pressed the tank handle with the other to drain it before it overflowed.

"Need some help with… uh… anything?" a sexy, male voice asked from the doorway.

"No," Georgia said, sarcasm dripping faster than the water off her face. "I thought I'd liven things up around here with a wet t-shirt contest this afternoon." Realizing her hand was still holding one wet boob, she removed it.

Grinning, he pointed under the tank. "I think that little silver lever thing down there turns the water off."

Did he think she'd honestly tear the entire commode apart without knowing what the hell a water shutoff valve was? "Are you sure?" she asked dryly, pissed at his condescension.

"Not really," her half-ass rescuer admitted. "I don't usually hang around when the plumber visits. I leave things to the experts."

"Good for you," Georgia declared, "but some of us have to fix our own toilets."

She bent and twisted the shutoff more, mad at herself when it turned easily a few more times. Great. She'd gotten soaked for nothing more than being careless. Luckily, Mariah hadn't tossed one of those damn blue cleaning tablets in the tank. That would have been disastrous. As it was, she merely smelled like chlorine. Her silk tank was likely a goner, but that couldn't be helped now.

"I didn't have the damn thing turned all the way off. Just my luck. First time I put on makeup in two weeks and now look at me…"

Then Georgia noticed the man had taken her up on her sarcastic invitation to do just that. He was silver-haired with just a few dark strands left, was sleek to the point of looking polished, and was wearing a watch that probably cost as much as her car. Every man that walked through the door of this place looked exactly like he did, only most were a lot younger.

She fought not to roll her eyes at him. "Here to see Dr. Bates?" Georgia asked politely, wiping her wet hands on one of the expensive paper hand towels Mariah kept stocked in her bathroom. They were ten times nicer than the bargain roll she kept at home, but they didn't soak up water any better.

Her half-ass rescuer crossed his arms, leaned in the doorway, and smiled at her with enough heat to melt a glacier. Probably paid a fortune for all those pearly whites too. At least he'd gotten his money's worth. The total effect of him leaning there looked as handsome as any slick magazine ad.

"I'm probably in trouble for dropping by without an appointment. I'd have been here sooner though if I'd known Dr. Bates was hosting a Friday afternoon wet t-shirt contest. You have my vote by the way."

Proving she was fundamentally still female enough to enjoy such nonsense, a laugh escaped her before she could stifle it with a frown. Georgia glanced down at her nicest white lace bra now showing through the evidently transparent-when-wet white tank. "Too bad I didn't wear the red bra today. All the boys love that one."

"I'm sure they do," he replied, not bothering to fight his smile.

Georgia shook her head. She doubted her breasts were anything like the perfect plastic versions the handsome man smiling at her was used to ogling, but never let it be said that she didn't have a sense of humor. She spread her hands, giving him a full view of her front. "Think these wet babies will get me a free drink or something?"

His masculine chuckle over her joke was delightful. The accompanying smile was warm and friendly as he nodded. A woman would have to be dead not to smile back and she certainly wasn't.

"Definitely *'or something',*" he answered huskily, "but I'd be happy to buy you a drink first. I'm that kind of guy. Why don't you toss on that cute sweater lying over by the sink there. I know this great Irish pub in Newport, lots of fun. We'll take a stroll along the Riverwalk afterwards."

Georgia deflated. Where the hell had this cocky older specimen been hiding a decade ago when she'd sorely missed sex and thought maybe she'd try finding someone to have it with again. Her arms lowered. He was a few years too late. Those urges didn't come anymore.

"You better let Dr. Bates fix you up with a newer model. I'm not your speed."

His genuine frown over her brush-off nearly made her take it back. He also looked way more disappointed by her refusal than he had a right to be.

"Are you sure?" he asked softly.

Ignoring his pleading gaze, Georgia nodded. "Yes. Tell Dr. Bates you want to date someone your own age for a change. A challenge like that should make her day."

He rubbed his nose with one hand and stuck the one sporting the expensive watch in his pants pocket. Georgia had never seen a man look so guilty, not even Ted that time he'd enlisted for two more years at that hellhole base she'd detested without first talking to her about it.

The man in the doorway suddenly blushed as

handsomely as any actor playing a role in a movie. That's when she figured it out. He probably did date twenty-year-olds. That's what well-preserved men like him always ended up doing. They didn't come looking for sixty-something widows like her.

Her self-preservation kicked in and rolled off her tongue. "Don't worry, Hollywood. There's no short supply of those young cuties you like in the world. My adult grandchildren are working on a baby girl right now. You'll only be seventy when she's ready."

Turning her back on the most handsome man she'd ever come across, because it was the only action that made any sense, Georgia picked up the new hose and sat on the closed toilet seat to finish her task.

"Hollywood?" he asked, ignoring the rest.

Not turning around for a last look, Georgia laughed off his question, the sound echoing inside the now empty toilet tank.

CHAPTER TEN

MARIAH SMILED AS DELLA USHERED THE VERY handsome plastic surgeon into her office. Brentwood Colombo had been married four times. It was easy to understand why. Outside of his woman centered profession, he had the kind of masculine confidence in himself that naturally drew women to him. Even Della beamed every time the man talked to her. A woman would have to be dead not to appreciate his appeal.

"Dr. Colombo, what a welcome surprise. What can I do for you?" Mariah asked. The man walked to the chair in front of her desk and let his well-kept body drop down into it.

"I've been coming here since you opened your doors, Mariah. Are you ever going to call me, Brent?" he demanded.

Mariah blinked hard at the question, not sure what kind of frustration she was hearing in his tone. "Of course. If it will make you feel more comfortable with me."

The silence grew as he leaned back in her comfortable guest chair and stared at her.

"I wasn't expecting you until next week. I don't quite have the next list of candidates put together for you..." Mariah began, stopping when he held up a hand.

"Forget the list. I have a different problem. Who's your plumber?" he demanded.

Mariah sucked in her bottom lip to keep from laughing. *Plumber?* Her favorite client wanted her to find him a plumber? She'd officially stepped onto the crazy train this week.

"Okay. That's not part of my usual services, but I suppose Della could make you a list of highly rated plumbers in Cincinnati. It shouldn't take her long. She's a whiz at googling things."

He was one of those men who looked even more handsome when he was confused. His wrinkled up face was adorable. No wonder he'd been married all those times.

"No, no. I want specific information about the one fixing your toilet. Do you know her?"

Mariah swallowed her shock while wondering what her mother had said or done now. "Yes. I know her all too well. Why do you ask?"

Brent Colombo steepled his talented surgeon's fingers in front of him and smiled. "I'll double your normal fee for a match if you get me a date with her. The woman interests me."

Mariah felt her mouth drop open, but couldn't stop it.

"Close your mouth, Dr. Bates. I promise you I'm not joking," he ordered.

"But..." Mariah said, stammering as she wondered how

to explain the truth to him. "She's not in *The Perfect Date* database."

Brent cleared his throat. "Yeah, she didn't seem like your usual type, but you can add her, right? Okay, here's how serious I am. I'll triple your fee."

Triple her fee? "Brent, getting set up here at *The Perfect Date*... well, it doesn't work that way. More money won't cause what you want to happen. I don't think a match with her is possible."

"Then I guess I should probably confess I asked her out already. I probably shouldn't have, but it just sort of slipped out in one of those moments that only come once or twice in a lifetime. It didn't occur to me I was breaking any rules when I asked her to dinner."

"You asked her to dinner?" Mariah's mouth dropped open again. She made herself close it. "What... what did she say?"

"She turned me down. I have no idea why." He frowned. "Are you worried she'll sue for harassment?"

Mariah chuckled. That was the best thing she'd heard yet. "No... no, nothing like that."

Brent gave a dismissive man grunt. "Good. She didn't seem the type. In fact, she had a great sense of humor."

"I don't understand your interest. She's *triple* the age of your last two dates," Mariah informed him as bluntly as she could.

"I know. That's why I offered you triple the fee for her. I stand by that by the way. Make sure she sees some of it. I think she might need a new car. Something she said made me think that."

Mariah shook her head, again wondering what in the

world her mother had said to her client. "I could never take your money so unfairly."

"You have to make a living, don't you, Dr. Bates? My money is mine to spend as I please."

Mariah held up a hand. "I'm not debating your client rights. But that plumber—that woman you asked out—she's not someone I hired. She's my mother."

She laughed softly when Brent blushed and rubbed a hand over his face. She was pretty sure he was swearing under his breath.

"*Your mother?*" he asked at last.

Mariah nodded, unable not to grin at his total surprise.

"I see. Does she fix toilets for a living?"

Mariah had to laugh at his obvious distaste over the idea. "No. Mom's a retired military wife. She thinks of herself as being resourceful. She was doing me a favor and trying to save me paying a plumbing bill. It's how she is."

Brent scratched his nose. "I see. Your mother. Is she married then?"

Mariah shook her head. "Widow. My father died a long time ago."

Brent stuck out his bottom lip as he thought. He laughed as he let out a long breath. "Wow, I'm sorry about your father, but her unmarried status is a big relief to me. I mean, given our exchange in the bathroom, I'd have felt kind of bad if she'd been married. Why did she say no to dinner if she's not in a relationship? I could tell she was interested in me."

"I have no idea," Mariah said truthfully, thinking Brent was the most confident man she'd ever met. Her mother might not have even heard his offer. Georgia

NEVER IS A VERY LONG TIME

Bates had a way of tuning out what she didn't choose to hear.

Brent snapped his fingers. "I've got it. Set me up on a date with her and I'll tell all my single friends at the *Smoking Loon* about your business. You'll have so many well-heeled male clients, you'll need two databases to handle us all. Now that's a deal you can't refuse."

The *Smoking Loon* was a prestigious country club in Hamilton County with an equally prestigious and pricey membership most people dreamed of bragging about having one day. Dan had wanted a membership there, and they might have gotten one eventually, but the club fees had seemed too excessive to her.

Mariah sighed over the loss of his recommendation, knowing she really could double her clientele with that kind of social boost. "That's a very tempting offer, but again, I'm going to have to decline. This is my mother we're discussing, not some random woman waiting for the perfect man to date."

She laughed when Brent crossed his arms stubbornly. She barely kept herself from rolling her eyes.

"Will you think about it a little longer before you give me your final answer?" he asked.

Mariah laughed full out then. You had to admire his persistence. Her mother would have a very hard time wrangling this man the way she had her Air Force father. "I can promise you I'll not be able to avoid thinking about it. I'm sure I'll get an earful from my mother too, as soon as you're out of hearing range."

"A whole earful, huh? Well, I guess I'd better get out of here then so you two can start talking about me. It's Friday, you know. Everybody should leave work early on Fridays. Playtime is important."

They hadn't really talked about the reason for his impromptu visit, but Mariah wasn't going to point that out. She was still trying to wrap her head around her mother charming Brent Colombo into asking her for a date. The idea was mind boggling.

She walked her handsome client out of her office where they found her mother sitting primly in the waiting area. Jackie O couldn't have looked more calm and collected. Her mother wore a new blue sweater and a pair of slim-fitted navy slacks ending at her shapely ankles. Topping those off were a pair of stylish, cute flats. She looked great except for the water stain on her no longer white silk shirt.

"Toilet fixed?" Mariah asked dryly, mouth quirking in humor when her mother glared at her.

"Yes, and I turned the little silver lever thing under the tank so the water came back on. Someone big and strong pointed it out to little old me."

"Silver lever thing? Are you talking about the water shutoff valve?" Mariah asked around a chuckle, wondering why her knowledgeable mother was playing stupid. She got her answer when Dr. Brentwood Colombo, who could undoubtedly pay people to flush for him if he wanted, huffed indignantly beside her.

Mariah was stunned when Brent walked to her mother who stood up immediately to head him off. They were nearly the same height, a fact emphasized by the eyeball-to-eyeball staring contest they were now engaged in. She heard Della nearly choke trying to restrain a giggle. Her assistant was getting all the dissertation research she was ever going to need from the lackey job Mariah had offered her.

"You're a very lucky woman for someone your age. You have the breasts of a twenty-year-old," Cincinnati's most renowned plastic surgeon informed a glaring Georgia Bates.

Her mother glared back at Brent, unmoved by the compliment as far as Mariah could tell.

"I'm sure you'd know all about twenty-year-old breasts, wouldn't you, Hollywood?"

Brent seemed undaunted by the mean in her mother's statement. Instead, he smiled at her... widely... showing all his perfectly white male predator teeth.

"That sweater brings out the exact color of your eyes. You look really cute in it... for a plumber," he said.

"Save your breath, Hollywood. I don't flirt with men whose watches cost more than my car."

"But you just did."

They both went silent after his last taunt, returning to merely glaring at each other again. Her mother broke the silence with a swear word—of course. Brent put his hands on her arms, leaned close, and whispered something low in her ear that made her mother frown hard.

Mariah would have given her next match fee to know what Dr. Brentwood Colombo had said to her mother.

She was so mesmerized by her mother swapping insults with a man that she didn't even jump when the now familiar, and still very sexy, male voice whispered softly in her own ear.

"Glad now that I stopped by to check on you. That's way more snap, crackle, and pop than I got out of my breakfast cereal this morning."

She turned her head and looked up, finding herself staring at a grinning John Monroe. "That's my mother," she whispered.

John's grin got broader as he snuck a look at the whispering older couple. "No kidding. Is the guy a client?"

"He has been up to now."

John's low chuckle over her mournful tone had the glaring pair putting some distance between each other at last.

"It was fun meeting you. See you later, sexy," Brent said, nodding at her mother before turning to leave. He paused by Mariah as he walked by. "Do think about what I said. I have an unlimited black card."

Mariah didn't answer, just closed her eyes. She could all but feel John shaking with laughter beside her.

How John managed to invite himself to dinner with her and her mother was as much a mystery as was why he was involving himself in her life at all. Yet for the third time that week, Mariah found herself sitting across a table from him.

It was the first time though that she was at least mildly happy about his pushiness. John's large distracting presence was keeping her mother's ranting about Brent to a minimal level, though that fact was known only to her.

She was sure the ranting Georgia Bates looked unhinged to the rest of the restaurant patrons.

"The smiling idiot even asked me out. Like I'd go out with a man who dates twenty-year-olds," Georgia finished.

Mariah looked at her frowning mother. "Yes, Brent told me he asked you out and that you said no."

"Brent? Is that his name?"

Mariah blew out a breath. Since Brent had outed himself in front of all three people at the table, normal discretion had already taken a hike. "His name is Dr. Brentwood Colombo."

"Doctor? Sounds more like a Detective."

"That's on TV, Mom."

"Yeah. I loved that show," John declared.

Mariah gave him a chastising look for interjecting, but it just seemed to make him grin harder at her. A deep dimple appeared in one cheek. John was obviously enjoying her mother's meltdown, as much as the steak in front of him. He was also enjoying seeing Mariah squirm on yet another professional hot seat.

"Brent seemed very sincere about his interest in you," Mariah offered her fussing parent.

"Tell me the truth, Mariah. How old was the last bimbo Hollywood dated?" Georgia demanded.

"I have no idea. There are no bimbos in my client database," Mariah hedged.

Then she remembered Beth Stanley getting by her radar. A resigned sigh betrayed her realization. Fortunately, her mother was too livid to notice. When John covered his grin with a big hand though, she kicked him under the table, uncaring of what role he played in her life if he was going to make fun of her. His grunt of pain distracted her mother for another whole ten seconds before she rounded again. John's scoot out of leg range was very satisfying.

"You're dodging the question, Mariah."

Mariah glared at her mother. "Because you know I can't tell you. Client matchups are confidential."

"Fine. Don't tell me. Why should you be loyal to me? I'm just your mother," Georgia declared, standing up. "I'm going to go check in with the old fool in the mirror. She'll tell me the truth. She always does."

"Mom…" Mariah began, but Georgia Bates was already stomping off.

"I see you got the stomping off thing from your mother," John said calmly, watching her exit as well.

Mariah nodded. "At least she wasn't cursing like a sailor this time. I'm pretty sure she was holding back because you were here. Mom probably has the wrong idea about you just because you showed up unexpectedly at the office on a Friday afternoon at closing time. Her assumption about our non-existent relationship is the only reason you're here eating half a cow."

"I know," he admitted.

John's genuine laughter after her glare over his admission brought a reluctant smile to her mouth. It had certainly been one hell of a week.

"I wish you'd just tell me what's going on. It would make liking you a whole lot easier. I want to like you, but you're not helping me feel good about that urge."

"You'd want to kill the messenger if I told you," John said, putting his attention back on his food.

"Would I?" Mariah asked with genuine curiosity.

John nodded. "Yes. But in the end, everything is going to work out just fine, because you keep doing the right things by the right people. You're a good woman, Dr. Bates. Your integrity shines brightly. Even your grumpy mother knows that. She's just mad at Colombo because she couldn't intimidate him into running away as easily as she wanted. Frankly, I think you need to set them up."

Mariah liked hearing him praise her integrity, but what did he mean by it? Two court cases in a month would make even a good person start doubting themselves.

And as for her mother...

"I'm a matchmaker, not a miracle worker. My mother would never agree. Besides, I have someone else in mind for Brent. She's mature too, but a bit younger than Mom."

John gave her a pained look. "Your mother looks great. I can see why Dr. Colombo would be attracted. She oozes self-confidence just like you do."

"And curses," Mariah added. "Mom oozes curses too."

John grinned at her. "You're just feeling negative after a tough week. Put the idea of your mom and Colombo on hold and give it some thought later. The attraction between them had the whole room vibrating. I can understand why people would pay someone to help them find that."

Mariah lifted a hand to stop him from talking. "Last year was so calm. Twenty matches I made got married. Twice that many are still together and still dating. My business grew by word of mouth alone and that felt amazing. Even with the ugliest divorce in the history of Ohio happening in the background of my life, I felt fulfilled in my work for the first time in years. In my gut, I knew I'd made the right decision to open *The Perfect Date*."

"From what I've seen so far, you're doing everything as right as it can be done. The cocky plastic surgeon hitting on your jaded mother is comic relief, but also a lesson in what love is really like, right? It isn't always convenient nor does it happen at the best of times. God knows, I'm learning that lesson right now. I keep chasing you down and inviting myself to dinner out of desperation to have at least a few positive interactions with you. My standards are pretty low. I just want you not to hate me."

Mariah didn't know what to say in response to John's admission, but hate was the last emotion she would have named about how she felt.

"Mom and Brent might actually be comic relief for me if I wasn't living with her. You see, I *know* I'm going to get the full rant later. Then I'm going to have to tell her that he's serious until she believes it. Brent is a man on a mission. He intends for wife number five to really be his perfect match."

John's eyes lit with humor at her revelation.

"And I can't believe I just told you all kinds of things I shouldn't have about Brent's motives. Are you one of the good guys, John? Because I'm starting to like you way more than I should."

Not answering, John picked up his glass of water, took a sip, and then to her complete surprise, set his water down before leaning over and putting his mouth firmly on hers.

After two seconds, the shock of being kissed wore off and Mariah melted into his lips sliding gracefully over hers. There was heat and caring in each stroke, and both in a balance she'd never had before, especially not in a first kiss. The quick nip of his teeth scraping her bottom lip as he broke contact brought on a full rush of arousal. She saw he knew it too, because John backed away faster than when she'd kicked him under the table.

"You make me want to cross every damn line in my life," John whispered. "Can I pay for dinner?"

Mariah shook her head. "We better keep this meal professional. It's about all the resistance I have left," she whispered back.

"Dutch tonight, then," John conceded. "Hopefully, this will all be over soon. I'll take you someplace great. You'll love it."

Once again Mariah had no idea what John meant.

How long was she going to let this nonsense of not knowing go on? It wasn't like her to let anyone keep her from knowing something. John kept hinting that she'd been dodging a mental bullet for a long time without realizing it.

Mariah could all but hear the mutterings as her mother lectured herself in the bathroom mirror. Yet wasn't what Georgia Bates had done that day the perfect example of a woman with some genuine personal power?

Her sixty-ish mother—the most unpretentious, self-sufficient woman Mariah knew—had charmed the pants off a handsome, uber wealthy, and highly appealing man who any woman in her database would kill for the chance to date. Her mother had even made him forget the real reason he'd dropped by the office.

Mariah didn't have to guess why her mother had turned down Brent's dinner invitation. Georgia listened to her instincts. Her mother didn't trust Brent because she'd instinctively known the man dated women a third his age when he damn well wanted.

Another thing her divorce from Dan had taught her was that not trusting a man was a very different state of mind than simply not being interested in him. Not trusting Dan had put her on guard and made her doubt herself.

Hadn't she lived in that soul numbing state for two years too long already? How much worse could the truth be?

Mariah's chin dipped to her chest as she thought about her options. John was not going to tell her anything. He'd made that crystal clear. His ethics seemed as iron clad as hers, so how could she fault him? Following her around was his compromise.

There was actually a simple, if a bit unethical, way for her to find out at least a little of what John and Dan were keeping from her. The question was did she dare to bend her own rules in her favor for once? God knew bending them for Dan had done nothing to improve her situation.

If Georgia Bates had ever doubted her husband, her bold, brassy mother would have done anything it took to get to the bottom of the mystery. She wouldn't have given what Mariah contemplated a second thought before doing it.

Not only did nice women not make history, they typically didn't solve their own problems either.

Looking at the handsome, unhelpful man finishing his steak, Mariah was suddenly very tired of being nice.

CHAPTER ELEVEN

JUST AS SHE WAS WONDERING HOW SHE COULD GET into the gated neighborhood, someone leaving it had looked at her Mercedes and immediately offered to help. While lying to kind strangers was another first for her, Dan's strangeness and John's secrecy about it seemed to require those drastic measures to surmount the obstacles.

Liking that rationalization—since sneaking and deceiving was something detectives excelled at—Mariah took getting into the elite neighborhood so easily as a sign from the universe that she was on the right path.

The house was less grand than she'd expected, but it was one of the biggest she'd passed driving in this far. Standing at the door now, Mariah practiced her carefully planned speech only to be completely thrown off course when a woman her age opened it holding a tearful baby in her arms.

"Can I help you?" the woman asked, sounding very tired and in bad need of a break.

Mariah's heart clenched in immediate sympathy. "I'm so sorry to bother you. I must have the wrong house," she said, making a cooing sound at the still sniffling baby. "Poor little thing. Is she having a rough day?"

"Teething," the woman said quietly. "Who were you looking for?"

"Beth Stanley," Mariah answered instantly.

"Can I ask why?" the woman asked.

"Sure. She's a client of mine and I haven't been able to reach her. I just wanted to make sure she was okay and that nothing was wrong," Mariah said, embellishing their connection.

"This is her house. I'm surprised my daughter didn't give you her married name."

"Gramma? Who's at the door?"

The tired woman turned and looked down. She smiled as she pushed back the little boy's hair. "Back into bed, Daniel. You're not well enough to be out of it yet." The woman turned back to Mariah. "I have my hands full. Daniel had his tonsils taken out a couple days ago. Been a champ about it until today."

Mariah stared in shock at the six or seven year old boy, glancing back to the baby girl in her grandmother's arms.

"Luray..." Mariah said aloud as the strange puzzle pieces of the last two years fell into place in her mind. "I'm guessing she'd be Beth Luray now. I didn't know it had actually happened."

Which was the truth. Dan hadn't told her a damn thing.

Mariah smiled softly as the older woman looked at her oddly, but finally shrugged. "Beth and Dan finally got married just before sweetness here was born eight months ago. I don't know why they waited so long. He bought her this house well over a year ago. Mothers are the last to know and Beth's not one much for sharing."

"I know what you mean. I have two grown children myself." Mariah forced herself to smile and not to show pain or panic. She'd save that for later—much later.

Numb to all but the growing realizations she was experiencing, she slipped one of her business cards from her purse. "Let me leave you this. You can just give it to Beth when you tell her I stopped by. She'll know immediately what it's about. Since she's married now, I guess I can delete her from my database anyway."

"*The Perfect Date?*" the woman read from the card. She chuckled as she looked at Mariah. "Using a matchmaking service sounds exactly like something my Beth would do, but probably just to irritate Daniel. She likes to keep her man on his toes. Does a fine job of it most days."

Mariah smiled sadly and thought to herself that Beth's strategy had worked better than the grandmother knew. Both Beth and Dan had played her for a fool.

The woman laughed as she remembered something. "That girl… I swear, I've never understood how her mind works. She and Dan were together for nearly a decade before they married. I think he was one of those guys unwilling to commit."

"As you can probably imagine, I see a lot of those in my work," Mariah agreed, waving a hand as she glanced away to keep from glaring.

She looked down once more at the sick little boy now leaning against his grandmother's leg. In another five years, he was going to look more like Daniel than Randy did. And Amanda… God, her soon-to-be-arriving grandchild was going to only be a year younger than the baby in the woman's arms. Her grown children now had half siblings. It was nearly unbelievable.

"Sorry to have interrupted your already stressful day. I hope your grandchildren feel better soon. Thank you for your time, Ms. Stanley."

"No problem, Dr. Bates. I'll tell Beth you stopped by."

"Thanks again," Mariah said, hurrying back to her car now and away from living proof of Daniel's infidelity.

The situation was worse… far worse… than anything she'd ever imagined. Her mother had been right about Dan's interest being primarily in her money. His shallowness wasn't excusable, but she could see why money was important. The man she'd divorced had a whole other family he needed to support.

Other things made more sense now too. Dan told her he had no money for upkeep on the house he'd won in the settlement from her. It was because Dan had used the divorce settlement to buy Beth Stanley a home. Upkeep of one pricey residence would be more than enough challenge for his Detective's salary, even given his seniority level.

Her shock over her discoveries was large, but it was hard to pinpoint the most appalling one.

She didn't really care about the woman who'd become a client under false pretenses.

She really didn't even care about the lies Dan had told her to hide his secret life all these years. If he could hide something this large from her, there were probably many more things she didn't know about.

But neither of those things bothered her. Instead, they were proving out what her gut had been trying to tell her— what Bill and her mother had suspected long ago.

No. The question Mariah was wrestling with the most was how could she take any action to protect herself, much less get revenge on her deceitful ex-husband, without becoming some sort of ex-wife monster who destroyed the lives of all four of Dan's children?

The little boy looked exactly like her ex-husband. He had to be Daniel's son. Her heart broke for her own children and the pain they would suffer when the truth came out... and it would come out. A second family wasn't something Dan could hide, despite how long he'd done so up to now.

Mariah drove blindly until she escaped the prestigious neighborhood. She made herself focus on the car and roads and all the people passing her, until she got back to the parking garage of her office building.

Then... and only then... did she lean her head on the steering wheel and let herself cry over being Dan's fool for so long.

Why? Why? Why had she not seen this sooner?

Not letting Bill investigate Dan back during the divorce was probably the dumbest decision she'd ever made. It would at least have kept her from ever accepting Beth Stanley as a client.

When the crying jag was over, Mariah raised her head and dug down into that reserve of strength her parents had made sure she'd developed. There were many decisions she had to make. The first was legal in nature which meant she had to talk to Bill again.

And Dan wasn't the only man keeping things from her. Based on the hints he'd been dropping, John Monroe knew about Dan and Beth Stanley. He'd likely known all along—even the day he'd met her. It was somehow worse to think she'd allowed John to get so close without working harder to find out what he was hiding. Wasn't John's presence in her life just an echo of her naiveté with Dan?

The only good news coming out of her discoveries today was that John's secrets no longer mattered. She blessedly no longer cared about the nature of his connection to Dan either. The only remaining problem was that she liked John—she liked him a lot.

It was long past time she knew what was really going on. Next time she asked, she wasn't going to let him get out of telling her.

INSTEAD OF MEETING BILL IN HIS OFFICE, MARIAH called him and drove by his house. Abby answered the door, hugging her and offering her tea before she even got inside.

Bill took a single look at her face and asked Abby if she could let them speak privately about a business matter while she made them all tea. Abby hustled away, blessedly not offended, because she trusted her husband.

Before, during, and after the divorce, Mariah had joked about missing the sex, but if there was anything of real value to grieve in her failed marriage, it was discovering her trust in her husband had not been worth her personal sacrifices.

Always blunt, Bill asked the hard question. "You look like hell. What happened?"

Mariah sat in a comfortable chair by Bill's comfortable fire. Bill's house was a real home with loving people who lived in it. She'd introduced the pair of them, that was true, but the love they had built together still thrived between them. And today was the first day she ever remembered feeling envious.

"I don't know where to start. How about with me saying Dan's remarried already."

Bill dipped his head and looked at his fire. "I'm sorry, Mariah. I know that must hit hard. I can't even imagine what learning it must feel like."

Mariah shook her head. "No, it's not his remarrying that's upsetting me. I found out Dan has fathered two other children. He has a fairly new baby girl, but the older boy is six or seven years old. Six or seven years, Bill. And the boy looks exactly like him. Dan had to be sleeping with that woman a long time. I don't understand how he could have been having an affair for years while I never knew it. Am I truly that clueless?"

Bill's heavy sigh broke across her rant. "No. Of course, you aren't clueless. You were being a trusting wife who loved her husband even when he wasn't being very lovable."

"The mother of those children is probably the reason Dan moved out of my bed. He probably didn't have enough sexual energy for both of us. In all the years Dan had to be away from me and the kids for any length of time, not once did I ever question where he was. Now I feel like such a fool. There could have been a dozen women for all I know. I don't get any of this… because *I know* I was a good wife."

Bill leaned forward, putting his elbows on his knees. "I really am sorry things have turned out like this, Mariah. I never guessed any of it either. Maybe I should have when Dan pulled away from our friendship. I made overtures, but he never responded. Eventually, I quit trying to be his friend."

Mariah shook her head. "You know what the worst part is? The mother of those children is Beth Stanley. That's who Dan has married. I left my business card with Beth's kind mother. I know that was poor form but don't lecture me— it's been my only act of revenge so far."

Bill sat back up. "Wait… let's stop being mad for a few moments and look at the facts. Your divorcing husband's lover signed up as your client and then brought falsified charges against your company? What was her motive for such an action? We're looking at possible extortion and collusion between Dan and her to get even more money from you. It also explains why he might be offering to get back together."

"Georgia Bates is going to love knowing she was so right about him," Mariah said sadly. "If I didn't already hate Dan, I would now because I'm going to hear about this from my mother for the rest of my life."

Bill chuckled. "Glad to see your sense of humor coming to the rescue."

Mariah waved a hand. "You know I'm right."

His nod was accompanied by a grin. "That certainly explains John Monroe's involvement with Dan as well.

Those bogus court cases Dan trumped up got noticed by the higher ups."

Mariah glared. "Glad you get the bigger picture. Why don't you explain John's involvement to me?"

Sighing in resignation, Bill cleared his throat. "Alright. I guess it's time. John Monroe works as a special investigator. I don't know John personally, but I know about the office he works for, and I'm not talking about his 'special assignments'. They call people like him investigative troubleshooters, but what he really does is internal affairs work."

Mariah shook her head without speaking. She had no idea why. It had to be some state of shock.

Bill went on with his explanation. "Until you told me the woman was Beth Stanley, I was only guessing he was looking at Dan. I'll also tell you how those things work. Once John gets enough evidence to build a solid case, heads will start rolling downhill until John's bosses get positioned to chop Dan's professional head clean off."

"Oh, dear God." Mariah rubbed a hand over her face. "Is it bad that all I can think about is the children? No real crimes have been committed yet have they?"

"You would know that better than anyone since all of them area aimed in your direction," Bill said quietly. "You have enough to bring a possible extortion case against Beth Stanley. Many people would for the trauma she and Dan have put you through. Something provable like that, especially if we handle it as a criminal case, would lead right back to Dan if he's truly married to her now."

"He also used the money he got in the divorce to buy her a house. I have no proof, but I'm fairly sure. He told me he couldn't maintain our old home and that he was going to have to sell it."

Bill grunted. "Legally, there's nothing we can do about that, but selling it would increase the odds of making all his motives towards you highly questionable. The investigation alone would be career damaging. What do you want me to do?"

Mariah sat quietly for a few moments, staring into the fire. Finally, she turned to Bill. "Nothing. I want you to do nothing."

Bill's grunt was short. "I like your attitude about forgiving and forgetting, but as your attorney…"

"Do nothing right now, except monitor the charges the former Beth Stanley, now *Luray*, have brought against *The Perfect Date*. Protect my company as best you can and make sure nothing remains of the allegations. I want my business to be above any reproach."

"Can I at least hire a private professional to validate what you found out today?"

Mariah shook her head. "Why waste the money? It would be redundant. Someone very professional already has all the evidence we need." She got up and reached out her arms. "Thank you for listening. The crying was helpful, but I'm much better now after talking with you. I needed a friend more than an attorney today."

Bill hugged her and rubbed her back. "You're a good woman, Mariah Bates. Don't let this bad stuff change you. It wasn't a fight you started, but it's one you can finish now whenever you want."

Mariah nodded. "Thanks. After I leave, tell Abby everything. I love her too and don't want her to feel like I'm keeping secrets from her about my personal life. I'd love to stay for tea, but I need to go home and tell my mother. I may have to tie Georgia Bates to a chair so she doesn't charge off to defend my honor. Wish me luck."

Bill chuckled as Mariah walked to the door. "Want some genuine friend advice with no joking around?" he asked.

"Sure," Mariah said, trying to be brave enough to hear it.

"John Monroe's been doing his job—a thankless one—this whole time. He honestly couldn't tell you and still do what he had to do in a fair and unbiased manner. If you'd said anything to Dan about what John was doing, even accidentally, it could have jeopardized any case John's office is building. Dirty cops don't need to be on our police payroll, Mariah. John's not the bad guy in this, so don't turn him into one. And here's the friend part... *don't* let your natural attraction to John be one more thing Dan takes from you."

Nodding once more, Mariah left, thinking exactly about that.

CHAPTER TWELVE

MARIAH LIFTED HER HAND TO KNOCK DESPITE hearing a man inside swearing about the ball game statistics blaring from the too loud TV. Before she fell too far down the "oh, he's one of those men" rabbit hole, she cleared her throat and readied her speech.

Twice in one day she'd managed to track someone down. Maybe she'd missed her calling. She wasn't half-bad at this covert stuff.

She knocked a second time. When that didn't get the door opened, she rang the doorbell multiple times.

"Alright. Hang on. I'm coming," an irritated voice called from the other side.

It was such a normal, disgruntled male reaction to having his ball game interrupted that Mariah couldn't help but laugh at the trouble she was causing. No secretive white knight in residence today. Just an off-duty cop trying to watch a freaking ballgame in peace.

Catching John doing something mundane and not

supercop-ish made Mariah hopeful. Of course, he could still send her away, but she wasn't going to look at the worst case scenario yet. She'd chickened out of going home to her mother, but she'd survived a lot of other emotional crap before deciding to show up here.

Tracking John down was a big risk—bigger even than tracking down the woman who'd slept with her husband. Bill was to blame for her standing in front of John Monroe's door while biting her lip because he'd been right about not letting Dan take this from her.

Blessed with being a mostly optimistic person, Mariah chose to celebrate the minor pain she was accidentally inflicting with her bad timing. She lifted a hand to hide her pleased smile just as John Monroe finally opened his door to her.

He looked exceptionally sexy in his black, wire-framed glasses, his faded Bengals shirt, and matching black sweats. Large bare feet poked out from the bottoms of them. No socks... which she found instantly endearing.

His unkempt appearance alone made it worth every cent of lost income she'd sacrificed to bribe Elliston to tell her where his uncle lived.

"Mariah?"

She smiled at his total shock and lifted her hands out wide. "In the flesh... last time I checked. I don't think I'm a zombie yet."

"What are you doing here... I mean, at my house?"

"Not sure yet," Mariah answered truthfully. "Got any company you're hiding in there?"

"In where?"

Mariah belly laughed at his confused question. "Have I shaken you up that badly?"

John rubbed his face. "Yes. You tracked me down."

Mariah crossed her arms and stared at him. "First time as the person being stalked? How does that feel?"

His grin began at the edges, and then he ran a hand through his hair making it stand up. "Why yes, Detective Bates. This is my first time to be stalked."

She lifted a brow and waited for a polite invitation.

"Oh, right. You want to come in?" John asked.

Her head bobbed. "Yes. I didn't bribe your nephew for your address so I could stand outside in your hallway. Should I come back after the game's over?"

John rolled his eyes at her sarcasm. "Of course not. Come in. I was just…"

Mariah stepped across the threshold and walked a few steps inside. "…relaxing," she finished.

He nodded and motioned down his short apartment hallway. "I thought you were the pizza I ordered an hour ago."

The doorbell rang on cue as if she'd planned it just to irritate him. "I've got change for a tip if you need it," Mariah offered sweetly.

Giving her a look that said smart-ass, even though he didn't call her that out loud, John answered the door again. He came back with a pizza and Mariah realized she hadn't eaten since breakfast.

"You're welcome to eat with me, but I have to warn you…"

"…the toppings are all meat and the only vegetable on the pizza is onion," she finished dryly.

John sighed. "Your comments manage to crawl up my ass faster than any person's I've ever met in my life. How *that* somehow turns into me frothing at the mouth to get my hands on you is still a mystery to me. I should be running like hell in the opposite direction."

"Or you could simply ask me to leave," Mariah suggested.

For a moment or two, John looked like he might do that. Her mouth twitched at the debate he was having with himself. It was happening in his eyes. If she grinned, it might prove to be his snapping point.

"If I promise to only eat one piece of pizza and not complain about anything related to your team, can I stay and watch the rest of the game with you?"

John nodded and she could tell he was totally out of his comfort zone. He was definitely not a person who liked surprises, but he was making an effort for her.

"I have wine," he said at last. "Just no rabbit food."

"It's okay. I didn't bring a rabbit," Mariah said softly, falling a bit more in like with him than she'd meant to.

Not commenting on her joking response, John used his unshaven chin to point to the apartment-sized couch he probably took up most of the space on. Mariah smiled and nodded, moving in that direction. He returned moments later with the pizza box, paper plates, and a bottle of red wine he'd opened in the kitchen. On a second trip, he brought back wine glasses, bottles of water, and napkins.

"We can turn the game off and talk," he said as he sat.

"No," Mariah said firmly. "I just needed to see you in person. The ballgame is good by me. I'm even giving you optimism points for wearing that shirt. I expected you to be more of a realist."

"I believe in loyalty," John said.

Mariah nodded. That had always been important to her too. Her celibacy had been sacrificed to the loyalty gods when she was trying to work through the problems in her marriage.

She opened the pizza box on autopilot and put food on their plates. Reaching over, she put a napkin on his knee, then handed him a plate.

"Eat. I'm fine," she said.

When she'd finished her slice of pizza, Mariah poured wine for both of them. Scooting to the edge of the small sofa, she pushed back into the corner of it and got comfortable. John was quieter than he'd been before she'd arrived, but at least she hadn't ruined the game completely.

She sipped her wine and tried to watch, but ended up watching John more. Her mind kept wandering to all she'd learned about her life. Suddenly, she felt like she was playing a game herself. She eased out of her cozy spot and set her wine down on the coffee table. It was probably best if she excused herself and left.

"Stay," John ordered, not even looking. "So long as you're not angry at me, I really don't care what brought you to my door."

"And that's why I noticed you. You're eerily observant," Mariah said.

"It's innate. My choices were cop or scientist. When I was growing up, geeky guys never got lucky with girls. I figured my chances were better in a uniform."

Mariah giggled and picked up her wine again. "As in football uniform?"

"You got it."

She laughed when the dimple appeared in his cheek again. "That's kind of sad. You could definitely make the whole white lab coat thing work in those sexy glasses you're wearing."

"Can't wear contacts all the time. Got to give the eyeballs a break. Science taught me that, but pretty much everything else came from football."

Mariah smiled at his efforts to tease. "I think you look cute in your glasses. You should wear them with all the confidence in the world."

John turned to her. "I think you look cute too, even if you have cried all your makeup off."

"A genuinely observant man. You do know you're a dying breed, right?"

John took her glass of wine and placed it on the table for her. He bent to the floor, slipped off her shoes, and then lifted her feet to his lap.

"Sleep. It makes everything a little easier to handle," John suggested, pulling a Bengals throw from behind him. He wrapped up her feet, then tossed the rest of it over the rest of her.

Mariah stared at his profile knew he was being careful with her... appreciated it even. "I'm sorry I didn't call first."

"I'm not. I'm glad you wanted to see me and made it happen. Just don't tell anyone you made the first serious move. I might lose my man card."

"If what I feel under my feet through several layers of blankets is any indication, I think your man card is safe."

His full belly laugh over her boldness was like winning the lottery. Despite his arousal, John got more lazily comfortable with her after that. He stretched out in her direction, sliding his long arm nearly the full length of the small couch. She wasn't exactly sitting in the circle of his arm, but she felt like she was.

She also felt wanted for herself. Their attraction had truly defied their sucky circumstances so far. She'd be the first to admit John's attentiveness was a healing salve to the wounds Dan's infidelity had created.

She closed her eyes, letting herself enjoy the feeling of mattering to a man, and fell asleep.

CHAPTER THIRTEEN

SHE WOKE SOME TIME LATER ALL WARM AND comfortable. John smiled down at her as she blinked up at him. His unshaven beard was nearly as silver as his hair. He really was incredibly sexy in those glasses. "How long did I sleep?"

"Through the rest of the game and a whole movie. The evening news is on."

"Wow. That's late." Mariah scooted to a seated position. John's fingers dropped to her shoulders, playing with the ends of her messy hair. "Some fun date I am."

"Was this a date?" John asked, his eyes crinkling behind his lenses.

Mariah groaned and closed her eyes. "I have no idea. It's been a very, very strange day."

"Is your mother going to be worrying about where you are?"

"That question makes me feel like a kid again." John

laughed as she rubbed her eyes. "I told her I was coming to see you and to not wait up."

John's fingers stopped what they were doing and his eyebrows went up.

"I was planning to sneak in after Mom went to bed so I wouldn't have to explain things to her yet. I'm still processing what I learned. Are you going to explain your role to me?" Mariah asked.

John pulled back his arm and blew out a breath. He nodded reluctantly. "If I have to."

Mariah chuckled at his flat tone and pulled her feet out of his lap. She stayed where she was though, and pulled her knees up to wrap her arms around them. The throw covered her bare legs and the bottom of her skirt.

"How about I start the discussion?" Mariah asked.

John nodded at the offer.

"I saw with my own eyes today that my ex-husband has a whole other family. The oldest child is old enough to mean Dan was cheating on me long before the divorce proceedings started. During the year we were living apart, he also got Beth Stanley—now Luray, according to her mother—pregnant a second time. They have a darling baby girl who was born during the year of our divorce."

"So it's true, he did marry her?" John asked.

Mariah nodded. "That's what her mother said. And he used the divorce settlement I gave him to buy her a very nice house in a gated community."

John turned and met her gaze. "How bad did all that bother you, other than kicking your ass emotionally?"

Sighing, she blew out a breath. "On a scale of mildly annoyed to completely devastated, the truth put me in the

NEVER IS A VERY LONG TIME

god-how-could-I-have-been-such-a-fool frame of mind. My mother is going to be the one devastated. For all his faults, my father was a faithful man who loved my mother madly. Now my children… well, I can't even think about them yet. Their reactions could be off any scale I can imagine."

"I'm sorry, Mariah."

Mariah shrugged. "Dan's betrayal didn't keep me from wanting to come see you. I consider that a positive sign. I hope you do too."

John reached out and took her hand. He squeezed it tightly. "I was married once. When I had to be away a lot for work, she found someone who wasn't gone all the time. Before that happened, though, we had a son together. Will is twenty-seven, a little younger than Elliston. I confess that I let work keep me from being there for Will as much as he needed me to be when he was growing up. We see each other, but we're not very close. That's all on me."

"My kids have the same relationship with their cop father. Side effect of the job, don't you think?"

"Or of not having the right priorities. I haven't had anything but casual relationships since that one time in my life. I think the longest I've dated a woman has been a few months. Seems it always fizzles out when I have to work on something like this case where I can't really discuss much. When things get tough, I let her go with no hard feelings. Less trouble that way."

Mariah nodded and squeezed his hand back. "In most relationships, things change very quickly. It's obvious you love your son. I bet he knows that."

"He says he does, but you know how guys are," John joked.

"I thought I did once. In fact, I'm supposed to be an expert on people," Mariah joked back. "Are you planning to let me go as easily as you did the others? Seems you could have asked to be reassigned. Why haven't you?"

John looked in her eyes for nearly a full minute. When he finally spoke, Mariah could tell he'd made some profound decision about her.

"The office I work for—really work for—assigned me to watch Dan. He's a good cop on the edge of going bad. Beth Stanley, on the other hand, could be considered a criminal for bringing false charges against your company. It's obvious both of them are trying to get into your wallet."

Mariah pushed her hair behind her ears as she remembered Bill's remarks. How could she feel guiltless about John if she prosecuted Dan? Beyond involving John further, there were also four other living-breathing reasons not to want any serious harm to come to her cheating ex-husband. There was no choice except to let Dan get by with hurting her one more time.

"Is there any way for Dan to keep himself out of legal hot water at this point?" Mariah asked.

"Why? You wanting to save him?" John asked in return.

Mariah unbent her legs and scooted closer, not letting go of his hand. "Anything I wish for Dan is because of all *four* of his children. They didn't ask to be part of this mess. They don't know their father is not being a good guy right now. Clawing out Beth Stanley's eyes or cutting off Dan's balls, while both could be satisfying, wouldn't help anyone in the long run. I also could say he indirectly brought me you, which is something I don't want to regret. By my estimation, the only evil Dan really did to me was take my money and be unfaithful. No divorce is pretty. Right?"

"No, it's not. I can validate that for sure." John grabbed her hand and tugged her closer.

She resisted but only enough to hold his steady gaze. "If I go after one or both of them, then I have the welfare of the children on my head, and a host of other things to contend with. Also, I won't be able to stalk you with a clear conscience like I did today. Do you want that outcome for us? Avenging all the wrongs might seem the right thing to do, but it would not in this case be helpful in resolving any of the real problems. I'd rather cut my losses on the money and the infidelity, especially if I can have this connection between us be guilt free."

John swallowed hard. "Come here, Dr. Bates. I need to hold you while I think about your argument."

Mariah started to crawl into John's lap, surprised when he easily lifted her across his legs. He wrapped his arms around her and kissed her cheek. He put his hands under her skirt, making her squirm from the pleasure it gave her.

They sat that way for several minutes while he thought about what she'd said. She was just about to talk when he finally picked up the conversation again.

"Technically, I don't have enough to fry the bastard yet. Dan's been skirting the illegal line, but he hasn't crossed it in a way I could recommend taking him out of his job over. You're right that my conflict of interest problem with you complicates things for me... and us. Me being involved with you looks just as fishy as anything Dan's done, but I can't seem to help myself. And yes, I could have asked to be reassigned, but then I'd have worried myself sick about what he might do to you. I wanted to throttle him the day he served you and was such an ass. I could only hope like hell you didn't believe any of that shit he said."

Mariah nodded and then laid her head against his shoulder. "If I have to pick which man to save in this scenario, I'd rather save John Monroe, even if it means asking him to let the bad guy get away this time."

His answer was an indignant grunt. It made her smile and want to laugh at her luck with men. Was she really thinking about getting involved with another cop?

"John? I'm planning to talk to Dan and see if I can't get him to stop taking legal potshots at my business. Bill says I already have enough to prove Beth Stanley is trying to extort me. Naming Dan in that suit would bring everything he did as a cop into question, especially if he has indeed married her. The threat of me bringing a criminal or civil lawsuit should be threat enough to get both of them to back off."

"And if talking to him doesn't go the way you think it will?" John asked.

Mariah shrugged. "Do you really want to play the 'what if worst case scenario' game tonight? Sitting in your lap is giving me a much better idea of how to make use of our time. I cried out my disappointment in the last man I cared about already. Don't make me cry about losing my chance with you."

She giggled when John bent and leaned his forehead against hers. His hungry, nearly desperate kiss after that was expected, but the power it had to move her was far more thrilling than she'd imagined it would be. His demanding kiss matched the excitement his hands were creating with all their exploration under her clothes. She drew the kiss out for both of them, pulled gently away, and then as gracefully as possible backed off his very appealing lap and everything in it.

"Let's go climb into that unmade bed of yours and be happy for a few hours," she whispered.

John narrowed his gaze as he let her pull him up. "My bed could be covered in an expensive comforter and have a dozen decorative pillows tucked neatly on it."

Mariah laughed. "I know. Morbid curiosity over your bedroom decorating skills is why I'm seducing you. I want to find out for myself if you have better taste in bed linens than I do."

John looked around, whipping his head left and right before grinning at her. "Seduction? Is that what this joking around stuff is? I'm more out of practice than I thought."

Mariah rolled her eyes and dropped his hand, only to squeal when John scooped her up in a fireman's carry over one shoulder. She was still laughing at his caveman action when they got to his bed. It was incredibly messy and just as plain as she'd known it would be.

"Ha! I knew it," she bragged, looking at the crumpled covers bunched in the middle of a large mattress. Nothing was tucked under the corners.

"Mind your bedroom manners, woman," John commanded, his large hand playfully smacking her bottom.

"If you think that's going to stop my mouth…"

"God, I sure hope it doesn't," John said sincerely.

She was still giggling over his flirty comment when he pulled off his sexy glasses, put them on the nightstand, and then finally, finally crawled on top of her.

It was the happiest Mariah could remember being in a very, very long time.

FULLY DRESSED THE FOLLOWING MORNING, WELL, except for her shoes which were still by the sofa, Mariah walked back to the bed with the sexy man still in it and scooted onto the edge until she could be close to him. With her muscles still protesting last night's activities, she bent one long bare leg to make herself more comfortable.

Biting her lip in a near star struck state, she stared at the surprisingly fit man who'd managed in one awesome night to restore the female self-esteem the last couple of celibate years had taken away from her.

John must have felt her intense gaze because he rolled his head and looked at her fully clothed body with both disappointment and disgust. "Oh. You're one of those hit and run women, huh? Just use a guy and move on. That will teach me not to open the good wine next time. I could have had a couple of beers and gone to bed alone."

Not in the least put off by his joking grumpiness over her leaving, Mariah leaned down, kissed his chest, his neck, and his bristled chin while he groaned, before moving to John's mouth for a true good morning hello.

When she broke away finally, her heart was racing and she was aching for him. His hand was in her hair and tightening with every second she continued to stare at him. If she didn't leave soon, he might not let her. She certainly wouldn't mind if John used that incredible body of his to persuade her to stay. Not at all. Not even a little bit. He was an ocean's worth of sexy in the sexual desert of her life.

"Just so you know, I normally hang around after such excellent debauchery hoping for more of it. Though I would expect you to make me breakfast afterwards. How much triteness can you handle this morning?" Mariah asked quietly.

"I don't know. Try me," John replied, huskily.

She felt him loosen his grip in her hair and run his fingers through it instead. She leaned her cheek against his stroking. "Last night was seven kinds of wonderful and then some."

His dimple appeared when he grinned, which made him seem boyish and carefree. Could she truly have this lightness of being with him? She sure hoped so.

John cleared his throat to speak and cupped her face with one large palm. "Last night was something I'd only managed to dream about until you came along. You've ruined me for all other women—and I'm not joking about that—not even a little. It would be terrible of you not to stay in my life. Aren't you feeling guilty now for getting dressed this morning?"

Mariah closed her eyes, wanting more than anything in the world to believe she really could be every answer to John Monroe's sexual dreams. Wanting him made everything she needed to do just that much more important.

"I'd like to stay, but I need to go talk to my mother. I'm also tempted to tell my kids and let them torture Dan for me. Then I'd have to deal with their emotional issues around him letting them down, and that might tempt me to change my mind about what I intend to do. To you, I may not seem angry at him, but believe me, I still am. I'm just working to make the big decisions from a place where I don't hurt anybody out of revenge or bitterness."

John scooted up and scooped her up. His bear hug threatened to break her, or at least rob her of breath. Lord, the man was strong. Which was very nice in bed. Going to bed with John again was something she was going to be thinking about the rest of the day.

"Just don't change your mind about us," he ordered… or pleaded… or both. Mariah honestly couldn't tell from his tone.

CHAPTER FOURTEEN

There was a definite déjà vu vibe happening this morning.

They sat in her mother's Florida room in the same chairs as when she'd first told her mother that Dan had filed for divorce.

"I'm so stunned that I don't know what to say. All this time, I just figured he was chomping at the bit to experience some sort of second youth or something. It never occurred to me Dan might have children with another woman. Did you have any idea?"

Mariah shook her head. "No, Dan having another family never occurred to me."

The question itself revealed her mother's shock. Oddly, it was helpful to see her mother react this way. If her mother had witnessed her meltdown yesterday, Mariah was sure she would have looked far worse.

"There's a boy of six or seven… and a sweet baby girl. The boy's name is Daniel and he looks just like him. He's married to their mother now, or at least that's what the grandmother said."

Georgia leaned forward in her chair, looking at her daughter's calm face. "You're awfully serene this morning. Did spending the night with John Monroe take the sting out of Dan's betrayal?"

Mariah shrugged at her mother's directness. "I won't deny it helped, but I will blame Bill for me going to him so soon."

Georgia rolled her eyes as she chuckled. "Girl, I wouldn't have bought that lame excuse when you were a teenager, and I'm not buying it now. Either you said yes to staying the night with the man or you didn't. I think I know my daughter at least that much."

Laughter rose in Mariah's chest. No one was more black and white in her thinking than her mother. "Bill said I shouldn't let Dan take my attraction to John away like he had taken everything else. That may be the best advice he's ever given me. Or at least I'm thinking that way today. John's a die-hard Bengals fan. You have to wonder when you learn something so sad about a man."

"I know you're teasing because you're still unsure. Are you falling in love with him, Mariah?" Georgia asked.

Mariah knew she meant John, not Dan. After what she'd shared, it wouldn't surprise her if her mother never uttered Dan's name again.

"Not sure about the big L yet, but I certainly do like him a lot. John's seen me at my worst and not gone running. There's definitely enough chemistry and attraction between us for me to protect our chance to pursue it. That's why I'm going to confront Dan about what I know. As ugly as the discussion might get, if he stops his harassment, it could make all this easier."

"Great. I think you should confront him. Want to take my gun with you?" Georgia asked.

Mariah snickered. "No, Mom. You know I don't like handling firearms. And I'm heading to his office downtown. You get a pat down when you go into an area with policemen."

Georgia scooted back in her chair. "Okay. What are you going to do if Dan gets snotty about being caught red-handed? He's done a bang up job of hiding everything up to now."

"I have one goal and one goal only. Kick Dan out of what's left of my life. Then I'm going to go to work at my business that he better leave the hell alone if he knows what's good for him."

Georgia chuckled. "In other words, you have no idea how you're going to handle it if he gets mean and pissy."

"You do know me well," Mariah said, rising to hug the good-humored woman who bore her.

INSTEAD OF HEADING TO DAN'S OFFICE, SHE'D GOTTEN a text from Elliston and swung by her office to see him. Della was already in residence and in rare form today. The woman tended to sport a very Goth look when she was dealing with negative personal stuff.

"Boyfriend problems this weekend?" Mariah asked.

"And that's why you get the big bucks," Della muttered

with a sad smile. "It's over and I ended it. I'm fine though. No need to concern yourself."

"Did Elliston let you know he was stopping by?"

Della shook her head. "No. The sexy geek did not tell me he was coming. What did he do? Text you for an appointment?"

Mariah nodded. "Yes, but he earned that right and more this weekend. I'll explain later."

Della chuckled. "If he's responsible for that genuine smile on your face, you need to give him a discount."

Mariah chuckled and wagged a finger. They both turned when Elliston came through the door.

"Morning, ladies," he said, grinning at both of them.

Mariah nodded to her office with her head. After they were inside, she closed the door. "Thank you for helping me find your uncle. Asking you for his address was the most unethical thing I've ever done."

Elliston chuckled. "It wasn't unethical. It was obvious to me that he liked you. Even Lynn noticed it at the fundraiser. Plus, Uncle John sent me a very interesting text this morning that confirmed everything."

Mariah felt her face heat. "He did? Oh, lord."

Elliston nodded. "All it said was—*thank you*."

Mariah sat in her chair, smiling as she studied the ceiling. "I'm surprised he was so nice. I caught him watching a Bengal's game."

Elliston burst out laughing. "I can only imagine how that went. He refuses to have company during game time."

"I got a pass because I slept through it all." Mariah felt the laughing young man's gaze on her face. "He did give me a piece of pizza and a glass of wine. Should I feel special?"

"Extremely," Elliston declared.

"What can I do for you, Elliston? I owe you one."

"Nope. We're even," Elliston said firmly. He pointed to himself. "I'm proud to say that you are looking at Elliston 2.0. That's what I came to tell you."

Mariah laughed at his description of himself. "Elliston 2.0. How so?"

"Lynn was great. The physical chemistry wasn't there, but the friendship was. It was actually fun getting to know her. I hadn't had fun with a woman in a long while. I also talked her into dating the younger man she's actually in love with, but had been refusing to date because of their age difference. It turns out Lynn and I were mutually good for each other. Except you're down one client now."

Mariah sighed. "That's too bad. I'll be very sorry to see you go."

"Not *me*," Elliston protested with a laugh, waving a hand. "Meeting Lynn made me optimistic. I'm more gung ho than ever to find my perfect match. I was talking about Lynn leaving you. She told me she spent the weekend with her very happy beau who now wants to meet me. It made me feel really good to know I'd helped them get together. I figure that's how you must feel when things work out."

Mariah smiled. "It is indeed. If Lynn is that happy, that's all I want… it's all I want for any of my clients."

Elliston nodded. "That's why I wanted to tell you this before I forgot how it felt to get things straight for once. I see people spending money all the time on expensive vacations, expensive toys, lots of things that don't bring them much satisfaction. I've done that mindless material stuff myself. Spending money to meet Lynn was great because meeting her helped me figure out what I actually wanted from a real relationship. In my opinion, your services are worth every penny. Next time I look at potential dates, I won't be looking at age or appearance. I'll be looking at the whole package. That seems a lot healthier."

Mariah sighed in satisfaction. "I'm so very glad you came to see me this morning. Your praise is the perfect start to my week. So are you ready to go back to the database again? It will be on the house this round. I really do owe you one."

Elliston grinned widely. "Let's hold off a bit. I've got a couple months of crunching to do. I got a lot of business after the fundraiser."

"More good news," Mariah said, smiling at him.

She walked Elliston out and accepted his masculine, cologne-scented hug when he offered it.

"Goodbye, Mr. McElroy," Della said politely.

"I'll see you in a couple months, Dr. Livingston," Elliston said, exiting as quickly as he'd arrived.

Della's sigh was not lost on Mariah. "Crushing on a client, Della? You can tell me. I won't have you flogged for it," she teased.

But Della shook her head. "No. Elliston McElroy just makes me hope one day I'll meet a guy that level and nice."

"They're out there waiting for you too," Mariah said confidently. "The trick is in finding them. Luckily, you work for an expert."

CHAPTER FIFTEEN

Mariah hadn't been to Dan's office years, but nothing had changed in all that time. No matter how many promotions he'd received, the atmosphere where he worked remained the same.

There was still the open room with desks crammed into rows. There was no privacy for most cops, but at Dan's level, he had his own office at least.

Yet that wasn't where she waited for him this morning. Dan's boss had put her into a conference room instead. Based on the security camera in the corner, and the total absence of the still secretive Detective Monroe, she'd guess John had already laid the groundwork for her not to be put into Dan's turf for their confrontation.

Dan walked into the conference room some half hour after she'd arrived, smelling like a million dollars, an irony that was probably always going to make her twinge. She'd given him half that amount in cash already. Once Dan sold the house, his share would have exceeded the amount she'd kept.

One day she was going to put all that aside. That wouldn't be today though.

"Mariah—what an unpleasant surprise."

The wry tone of Dan's greeting packed an odd blend of resignation and defensiveness in it. Mariah dredged up a polite smile, determined to be as fair as possible. "Did your new mother-in-law tell you and Beth I stopped by?"

Dan simply nodded at the question and slid into one of the seats at the table. Mariah continued to stand... and to wait for him to really answer her.

"I know you're not going to believe this, but I honestly never meant to hurt you. Everything I did was to preserve what you had achieved."

Mariah rolled her eyes. "You sent the prosecutor's office after my new business... twice."

"The second time was Beth's idea. I tried to stop her."

"How stupid do you think I am? You showed up to serve the subpoena for records yourself." She couldn't believe Dan had the gall to shrug at her statement.

"I really was trying to help you with my advice. You gave up a job that made you more money than you could spend in a lifetime. Why would you throw all that away? I'd have stayed if you'd kept your job. I never would have married Beth."

His insane rationalization over his infidelity exceeded anything she'd expected of him. Mariah threw up her hands. "Why would I want to stay married to someone who left me for another woman? Do you think I'm that desperate?"

"No. I think you're that smart. You know I was good to you and the kids," Dan said.

"Speaking of *our* children. Do they know you've remarried? Do they know about your other children? Do they know their father is a lying, cheating douchebag?"

Dan's sigh was large. "I was going to tell them about Beth and the kids eventually."

"When?" Mariah demanded. "When the new Daniel junior started college?"

"You don't understand," Dan said tightly. "This is your fault as well as mine."

"*My fault?* How in your warped mind does your cheating with another woman, and keeping a whole new family from me, equate to being my fault?" Mariah glared.

"All you ever did was work, Mariah. We made gobs of money and all you ever wanted to do was spend time with the kids and our loser friends. We could have done anything. We could have taken trips and drove fun cars. We could have really lived. You wouldn't even buy a country club membership even though you made more money than most of the members."

"My mother was so right about you. The only reason you stayed with me was because of the money. I think I hate you most because Georgia Bates is never going to let me live this down."

"Your mother is some piece of work alright. I always figured she'd be the one to find out. Your sleuthing skills surprised me. Knowing you saw the kids made Beth have to take a sedative to sleep. She's been dreading what you would do when you discovered them."

Mariah crossed her arms. "What have you done to the man I married? He was not this shitty of a person."

Dan laughed, even more amused. "Oh, I'm still here, honey. You're just mad at me."

Mariah snorted. "No. You've turned into someone I don't recognize. You even offered to take me back when you knew damn well you'd gotten remarried. That's disgusting, Dan."

Dan shrugged. "What can I say? I miss sleeping with you. Beth's exciting, but she has very expensive tastes. It's all I can do to keep up with her. You're my speed. It would have been nice to have our old life back too. I don't see why this is such a big deal. It only bothers you because you found out."

He was a narcissist. That was the only explanation. Had Dan always been one? Or had he become one somewhere along the line and she'd missed the change happening?

Mariah paced, staring at the floor as she walked. She was grateful there was a conference table between them. She was also grateful she hadn't brought her mother's gun because Dan's blasé attitude about screwing her over would have sorely tempted her to use it on him.

"Finding out you lied and cheated only validated the end of what we had. We've been divorced nearly a year now, Dan. I've moved on," Mariah said bitterly.

Dan laughed at her statement.

"What was the laugh for?" Mariah asked.

"I had John Monroe following you for weeks," Dan said. "He already confirmed there's no man in your life."

Mariah ran a hand through her hair, glared at her arrogant ex-husband, and bit back the brag she could have made. But no. She wasn't going to let Dan force her to go there. Her relationship to John would not become fodder for this hateful debate.

"That brings up another good question. Why did you have Detective Monroe following me?" Mariah asked.

"For evidence that doesn't matter now," Dan said tightly. "Beth's already withdrawn her case. You beat mine in the ground early on. Congratulations, Dr. Bates. I've given up trying to save you from yourself."

Mariah held his gaze. "When I came in here, that's all I wanted—just for you to quit harassing me. Now I'm not sure that's good enough. Bill advised me to counter-sue to protect myself and my business. He says I have enough evidence to bring a criminal case against Beth for possible extortion. The children are the only reason I haven't filed yet."

Dan shook his head. "You're bluffing. Suing is not your style. That would be very bad PR for the kind-hearted Dr. Bates."

"Bad PR?" Now it was Mariah's turn to laugh. "You've betrayed our marriage and the family we created together. You've been part of two wrongful court cases against me which is evidence of your collusion with Beth. Did it ever occur to you that your actions might at some point have some consequences for you as well? If you and Beth Stanley do anything else to me, I promise you that I'll make sure you get investigated by your superiors… and *she* will go to jail. Her mother's probably already raising the kids anyway. I saw the truth with my own eyes, Dan. And I'm done being nice."

"You'd never do any of that stuff," Dan said firmly.

Mariah barked out a harsh laugh. "Watch me. Next time I go to court, I promise you it will be you or Beth or both of you in the hot seat—not me. And you're already being investigated. Do you honestly think your currently sketchy reputation can stand up to the bad PR I can bring to you? I don't."

"Nothing from one of Bill's private investigator flacks is going to hurt me."

"No? Then how about the stuff your fellow cops will find out when they get involved? How about the prosecutors you've been bullying around to bring bogus cases? Think their office will help? You're ruining yourself, Dan. Technically, all I need to do is wait for you to implode your own career."

Mariah could tell the moment she got through his shields. She stared at him—stared hard at the stranger that the man she'd once loved had become. There was nothing left in Dan's face or his eyes that seemed familiar to her. There was certainly no regret for how he'd treated her reflected there.

Dan had become very much like the woman he'd chosen over her, but thank God it wasn't her job anymore to save him. What she'd said to him was truer than Dan knew. She really had moved on.

"You're all but gloating and that's not like you. What do you know that you're not saying, Mariah?"

Hearing the worry in his voice was surprisingly reassuring. "I know you need to leave me and my business alone. I know you need to watch your back and get your life straight. You're not nearly as insulated from your actions as you want to believe. I also know that the last money you're ever going to see from me is whatever you get from selling the house. You better make that money last for the rest of your life, Dan. When that's gone, it's all gone."

Dan rose from his seat. "Fine. We have Amanda and Randy to think about. Things don't have to get ugly between us."

Mariah glared. "They're already ugly and that's your fault. So if Bill brings one suit, I'll make sure he brings as many as I'm entitled to bring. I'll ask for the house back in lieu of other payment. There's no way you or Beth will be able to come up with the large amounts I'm going to ask for to make up for all the pain and suffering you two have caused me. Then you can see how your new expensive wife handles living off a cop's salary. We'll also see how your department handles learning the truth about their golden boy detective. I'll feel a bit bad to ruin your reputation and your new life, but I guarantee you that I will not regret one moment of protecting my own assets."

Dan rubbed his jaw. "You make a very interesting bitch, Mariah."

"Thank you. My once loving husband's betrayal did this to me. You can consider dealing with my vindictive side to be the first consequence you need to face," Mariah said sharply, wincing when Dan slammed the door on his way out.

Mariah glanced up at the blinking light on the security camera, hoping someone really had been recording it all.

CHAPTER SIXTEEN

"Did I shock you speechless, Della? I know it was a lot to hear. I don't even know if anything I said will do any good or not, but I'm guessing it will because Dan's boss is now involved. I'm pretty sure they recorded our entire conversation."

Della nodded from the chair. "I've always admired you, Mariah. It was mostly for the matter-of-fact way you would advise your radio callers to take action. Your sympathy was laced with insisting they take ownership for their decisions and choices. That's the kind of helpful doctor I want to be."

"Dr. Livingston, you will be exactly the kind of doctor you choose to be," Mariah assured her. "I just hope you don't think I've turned into some awful woman."

Della laughed at that coming from the most polite, warmest woman she'd ever met. "No. You're as nice as ever. I'm guessing some tall, silver-haired man helped you get over your evil ex. Detective Monroe looked quite capable of making a woman forget everything but him."

Mariah laughed. "You know I'm too honest to deny it, but I'm not certain our chemistry will last either. John's another cop in my life. It's not like I have any ignorance cushioning the reality this time. I'm like those women who end up dating only military men. Being attracted to cops is obviously a defect in my character that I can't find the source of."

Della smiled. "Can I just say then that Detective Monroe is better looking than your ex?"

"You may. He's better in bed too—way better—like a whole different kind of better," Mariah teased.

"Lucky, lucky you," Della said happily. "Having watched your relationship with John Monroe blossom has made me hopeful. Think my perfect match will show up in time for my baby sister's wedding this summer?"

"If not, I'll get you a date for that," Mariah promised.

"Great. I want Elliston McElroy—if he's still single then," Della said, giggling. "I'll put him in jeans and make sure his tats show. My family will be stunned by the way he looks and they'll stop shoving stuff-shirts in front of me. They still buy into the oldest child needing to marry first. Since I'm now going to be the last to marry, I've been a complete disappointment to them."

"Twenty-seven is still very young. My son is your age and not married."

Della lifted her hands. "I know. Right? My sister is nineteen. That's practically still a baby."

"Nineteen?" Mariah exclaimed. "Wait… Amanda was twenty when she married. Never mind. Love is all that matters. Georgia Bates taught me that."

Della's face brightened. "Right. Your mom. Speaking of her... are we fixing up her with the dreamy Dr. Colombo?"

Mariah shook her head. "No. I'm thinking about Ann Lynx. She's a better fit for him. They'd look quite elegant next to each other."

Della snorted.

"What? What was that sound about?" Mariah asked, laughing. "Are you actually disagreeing with me?" She watched her assistant grin while she pretended to think.

"Yes, Dr. Bates. Sadly, I believe I am. Chemistry like theirs is too strong to be denied. I think you should talk your mother into dating Dr. Colombo."

"Can't. My mother's still mad about him dating younger women."

"Just proves I'm right about the chemistry. If she didn't care, she would have forgotten all about him by now," Della insisted.

Mariah rolled her eyes, but then shrugged. "Let's try Ann first. If I'm wrong, I'll work on my mother next."

"You're never wrong about potentialities, Dr. Bates," Della said as she stood. "Seeing your mother and Dr. Colombo as a perfect match is as difficult as seeing you and John Monroe as one. I'm very proud of myself for seeing it before you did. I think you're in a strange mental place about love because of all you've been through the last couple of years. But you've got me. I'll be optimistic enough for both of us and keep my eye on the clients."

Mariah leaned her elbows on her desk. "I don't know how I'm ever going to run my business without you."

Della's smile was wide. "How about I work as your partner one day? Then you never have to."

Mariah blinked and straightened. "That has possibilities, especially if we keep growing. We'd need to hire another assistant."

Della shrugged, grinning over the enormous ground she'd gained. "I'll find us one. You can trust me to pick someone good."

"I do trust you," Mariah quickly agreed. "Let's talk about this again after you finish your book and get tenure. You can intern with me before your licensing just as well as at any clinic in town. I may have to list us in some database to make that happen. I need to think about this—get it worked out. Glad you brought it up now."

Della smiled and nodded. Consideration was enough for the present. She had learned the hard way to be patient. She hoped for Detective John Monroe's sake that he had learned that lesson too.

CHAPTER SEVENTEEN

"Mariah? I hate to bother you, but we have a visitor."

Mariah lifted her head from her computer screen and glanced at Della standing in her doorway. "I wonder how long it's going to take for me to quit reacting so badly when you say my name that way." Della's instant grin eased her mind. "Let's try this again... *who is it, Della?*"

"Detective Monroe is here to see you. He's not wearing a suit so I took that as a good sign. Can I send him back to see you?"

Mariah smiled. "Yes, Della. You can definitely send Detective Monroe to my office."

With a quick grin, her assistant disappeared, and moments later a large bouquet of red roses entered the room. Attached to the large handful of roses was a handsome, smiling man wearing his black wire-framed glasses, dark jeans, and a red Henley that showed off some of the best parts of his great body.

Mariah stood and walked around her desk. "Hello, Detective."

"Now don't start that again," John ordered, handing over the flowers.

Laughing at their private joke, Mariah stuck her face in the flowers and inhaled. "They're beautiful."

"So are you," John said, reaching out to touch her face. "Can I kiss you hello?"

Mariah smiled. "Best offer I've had in days."

His lips moving over hers was just as thrilling as it had been the first time.

John broke their kiss to speak. "I thought I'd come see if you wanted to have some dinner."

"Can we do that out in the open now?" Mariah asked. John raised an eyebrow at the question. His action made her laugh. "You know it's a legitimate question."

John shrugged. "Not after what you did to your ex-husband. He's been given an unofficial warning which I have on good authority scared him enough to take what you said very seriously."

"And just how do you know what I said?" She rolled her eyes when John looked sheepish. "Let me guess—the camera in the conference room was recording us the whole time."

"Yes, and I was in the room where the video feed was going. I can't believe you managed to call him an ass without using the word. I'm not counting 'douchebag' against you because that's merely an accurate description. Want a copy of it? Your mother would probably enjoy watching it. Maybe even your attorney friend."

Mariah groaned and hung her head. "No, thank you. I just want to forget about it. Did I blow your cover story?"

"No, but they didn't believe me. I took a two week suspension though, which shut them right up."

Mariah felt her mouth drop open. "Two weeks without pay for collecting a tape of me and Dan illegally?"

John shook his head. "No… and no one did anything illegal. The suspension was for telling my supervisor that I was involved with you. When I refused to back down from dating you, he threatened me with a two week suspension. It seemed a small price to pay—pun intended—for a chance to sleep with you again."

"But two weeks, John? That's half your salary for the month."

"Yep. Worth every penny," John declared. "So how about dinner? I feel like celebrating."

Stunned, Mariah nodded. "Okay. Sure. I'm buying until you go back to work. Let me get my jacket."

JOHN DROVE A LARGE MERCEDES, LARGER THAN HERS. It was silver and sleek, and seemed to oddly suit him in a way she couldn't identify. He was very much at home in it.

"Nice car," she observed.

"It is. Doesn't look fifteen years old, does it?" he asked.

Mariah shook her head and smiled. "No. It looks great —well loved and cared for."

"I take great care of everything in my life. Probably just another aspect of that loyalty thing you seem to like so much."

Dimple showing because of his wide grin, John glanced at her to see if she'd gotten his obvious innuendo. The wickedness lightning his eyes made her want to pinch herself to see if this happy moment was really happening.

He drove into a gated neighborhood she'd never visited before, pausing only long enough to key in a code which he did from memory.

"Is there a restaurant in here?" Mariah asked, knowing there wasn't.

"Something like that," John said mysteriously.

Mariah snorted and rolled her eyes. "Let me guess. You're one of those men who think women should squeal over every little surprise, aren't you? I am not a squealer, John."

"Squealing is mostly overrated," John said, grinning still. "And I have to disagree with your assessment. You do sometimes squeal."

"Ha. Ha," Mariah said dryly, but a feminine smile as wicked as his masculine grin plastered itself to her mouth.

They pulled up in front of a sleek brick ranch on one of the older streets. John parked and pointed at the house. "It doesn't look like much on the outside, but the inside is very nice. There's a great deck off the back too."

Mariah wrinkled her forehead. "Whose house is this?"

His shrug revealed nothing which is why his statement stunned her.

"This is the house where I was raised. I wanted to show it to you."

Mariah raised an eyebrow. "Are you planning to introduce me to your parents already? Moving a bit fast for me there, John."

His laughter rang out in the car. "They're in Florida, Dr. Presumptuous."

Mariah laughed. "What would you have thought if our roles were reversed?"

"Same damn thing," John admitted, opening his car door.

Mariah climbed out and followed John up the walkway. He used a key from the same fob as his car and opened the door. She walked into a mission styled home that Frank Lloyd Wright might have designed. The effect of the light on the polished wood was wonderful. Her nose lifted in the air. What she smelled was wonderful too. It reminded her that she was starving.

"Someone making us dinner?" Mariah asked.

John hung his head. "Sort of. I don't cook. But there's this guy I know who does takeout meals. All you have to do is pop them into the oven. It's healthy and good."

"Smells fantastic," Mariah admitted.

"Not as good as you do, but I'm trying to control myself."

John walked off after dropping that little bombshell, leaving her with the choice to follow his cute jean-covered butt to the kitchen or not. Rolling her eyes again, even though it made her feel like her mother, she tagged behind him like a puppy.

She walked into a kitchen that was warm and inviting. All the modern conveniences were there, but so was the lovely polished wood that made it seem substantial and like a home. It reminded her of Bill and Abby's place.

She looked at John, who was checking the progress of their dinner and at the open bottle of red wine on the counter. It was the brand she'd ordered the night he'd invited himself along to dinner with her mother.

"You really do pay attention, don't you?" Mariah asked softly.

John poured her a glass, turned, and carried it to her. "I think I've only been that way with you. I have a driving need to please you any way I can. I like you, Mariah Bates. And I'm falling in love with you—or have fallen. I haven't figured out which yet."

Mariah took the glass from his fingers and set it aside. She looked up into his earnest face. "I like you too. I'm afraid of the big L and I don't know when I'm going to get there again."

"I get that," John answered, holding up a hand. "But I want to be optimistic, so I'm going to buy this house. My parents are practically giving it to me because they want to stay in Florida. They shouldn't be home to visit often, but they'd stay here when they did. All the rest of the time, I'd be living alone. Only I don't want to be alone. I want to live here with you."

Mariah looked around at the well-used, well-loved, and well-preserved space. It was just happening so fast. She pushed a hand through her hair as John pushed out a breath.

"Look... I know this is ridiculously aggressive, but I was kind of hoping you would move out of your mother's place and move in with me. I'm not as wealthy as you, but I'm pretty sure I could give you a nicer life than you've ever had. I can afford this house and to feed you without even trying hard, especially since you seem to eat mostly rabbit food. I also know I will be the most faithful man you could ever hope to find. What do you say, Dr. Bates? Do I sound like your perfect match?"

Mariah picked up her wine, walked to a leather barstool, and slid onto it. She stared at John as she sipped. "What kind of proposal is this exactly? I'm... confused."

John shrugged. "Beyond being a desperate one, I'm not sure. You could probably call this anything you want. My instincts are screaming 'THIS ONE' and I have no choice."

Mariah laughed. "THIS ONE?"

John nodded. "Yes. Aren't yours screaming too? I figured you'd have never slept with me otherwise."

"But..."

John held up a hand. "I'll even let you put a whole comforter ensemble on the bed—any color you want. Twelve pillows and all."

Mariah laughed. She couldn't help it. "Decorating the bed would normally be my first concern in taking a new man on, but surprisingly, I'm more concerned that you could lose your job over me."

John nodded as he frowned. "Yeah, I knew that would bother you. There's several security companies who would take me on if anything like that happens, but I doubt it ever will. I'm never going to be out of work for long. One day I might have to retire to body guard my famous wife..."

"*Wife?*" Mariah sputtered, throwing up her hands in disbelief. "I thought you weren't sure what kind of proposal this was."

"That was twenty minutes and a lifetime of frustrated relationships ago. I've been sure since you handed me my balls that day in your office. I just haven't been able to figure out how to make it sound less insane that I feel that way. I'm not a complete idiot. I realize we barely know each other."

"But…"

"Look, your office is twenty-five minutes away. How about a probationary period? You can even have a separate bedroom like a roommate would, but I'm probably not going to let you sleep alone very often—if ever. I need you. And I've never said that to any woman before you. If you're around me, I'm going to be hitting on you—like all the time."

Her sigh was loud and rippled the wine in her still nearly full glass. "You need me?"

John nodded as he walked toward her. "Yes. You make me feel alive. You make me smile. You make me want to drag you off to bed every time I see you. At my age… well, that's a freaking miracle. I haven't wanted a woman like this since I was in my twenties. This is what a great relationship is supposed to feel like. Keeping you is worth whatever it takes."

Mariah groaned and put her head down on the counter. "But I hate all men right now."

"No you don't," John said tersely. "You hate yourself for being so wrong about your ex. Get over thinking you made a mistake, which you didn't because you got conned by a cop gone bad. When you accept that, you can let yourself fall in love with me. I promise—I truly am your perfect match."

"My perfect match," Mariah repeated.

John nodded. "You have no idea what that means yet

and I can't wait to show you. You're like a complete do-over for me."

Mariah blinked as she stared at him. Maybe John was her perfect match... but another cop?

That was just asking for more trouble, wasn't it?

"Look. I always put the toilet seat down, but I'll shave and shower in the guest bathroom if that's what it takes. That way you can spread your acres of girlie stuff out everywhere in the master bathroom."

Mariah chuckled. "I do not have acres of girlie stuff. I have a few things."

"Okay," John said agreeably, pulling out his phone. "Let me just call your mother and validate how many *things* you have with her before I apologize for jumping to conclusions."

"Cheeky smart-ass," Mariah declared.

"Cheeky smart-ass who's in love with you," John said.

Mariah giggled. "Okay, already. I'm convinced. I'll move in with you... eventually."

"Good."

"You have to settle for the little L until I can feel the big L though."

"Fine. That gives me a goal. Does the little L come with bedroom benefits?" John asked.

"Sure. I'll happily help you decorate the bed, though from what I see, your mother has great taste," Mariah said, laughing at the disgusted look he gave her. "I'm teasing, John. You're all I've thought about since we were together. I don't care what the bed looks like."

"Good. Now here's the toughest question... can you wait

to eat dinner? You're all I've thought about as well. In case there's been any gaps in your education, thinking hot thoughts about women is torturous for men in my love-sick condition."

A giggling Mariah slid off her stool. She walked toward the new man in her life who was soon to be her future. "I'd love to stay for dessert. Maybe even breakfast."

"Definitely breakfast," John said, sliding his arms around her waist and pulling her close.

He bent to kiss her, his lips demanding and grateful on hers.

EPILOGUE

MARIAH LIFTED HER HEAD AS HER ASSISTANT WALKED into her office. Della gave her a wicked grin before sliding into the seat in front of her desk.

"Can I just say I love my job?" Della asked. "Or do you have to know why?"

Mariah laughed. "You already know the answer to that."

Della giggled as she motioned to Mariah's neck. "You have love bites all over you."

Mariah tried unsuccessfully to look at them. "I do? I didn't even notice when I got dressed."

Della grinned as she sighed. "You sincerely inspire me not to give up on men."

Mariah looked back and smiled. "Good. Let's hope our clients feel the same." She glanced around the office. "I'm so glad I didn't let Dan take this from me. Last month I was miserable. Now I'm happier than I dreamed I'd ever be again. You really can't take anything for granted."

"At any age," Della added.

Mariah nodded. "Right. At any age… and speaking of age…" She pushed a stack of signup packets across the desk.

"Wow," Della exclaimed, sliding them toward her. "How did I get so far behind? Usually, I'm better about keeping up."

"I took a long time to decide which to add. The group contains eight new females for the database, but there are no fees for them. I'm picking up all the costs."

Della winced and made a face. "Pricey."

Mariah nodded. "Call it an investment. They range in ages from forty to sixty-five. They're the sassiest women I know."

Della flipped through and then laughed. "I would certainly put your mother in that category."

Now it was Mariah's turn to wince. "Yes. I had to put her in so her three best friends would sign up. They really are perfect for this, but Mom's not happy with having to play along. It's her fault for meddling instead of letting things go."

"Your mother does it for the fun of causing drama. Isn't meddling what we're doing at *The Perfect Date?*" Della asked, head down as she studied the bios. "The difference is people pay us big bucks to officially meddle in their love lives."

Mariah laughed. "I suppose we do meddle."

"With the best of intentions though," Della added. She looked up. "So are we hooking up your mother and Dr. Colombo?"

Mariah sighed and leaned back in her chair. "Mom

won't even have the discussion. I'm going to run Ann Lynx by Brent and see if that takes. She's a lovely woman."

"Lynx?" Della thought for a moment. "I went to high school with a Megan Lynx."

"Ann's her mother."

"Megan was very… tomboyish. Not in a bad way, but she just didn't have much time for girl stuff. Is she still like that?"

"Former Marine."

"That does not surprise me," Della said. "Bet she was a kickass one."

"So I hear. She married Nicolas North."

"That was *her*? Wow." Della exclaimed. "Her brother's a looker too, but he's all about that girl he met in college. They've been together for years. Why are all the good ones taken?"

"They're not," Mariah said, believing it completely. "But you have to put yourself out there. You also have to have the right frame of mind to let them into your life. I almost didn't let John in. That would have been very bad."

"Your love bites agree with you… and so do I."

Mariah laughed, feeling seventeen again. John really had given her a whole new perspective. "Ann is lovely. She's very pretty, teaches yoga, and takes wonderful care of herself. She could easily pass for a much younger woman. I want her to be one of the first to get her makeover, but she will insist Mom go as well. They're pretty tight as friends."

"I'm good with handling both at once," Della said.

"Thank you, Della. Thank you for sharing this journey with me."

"Just keep thinking of it as you training your new

partner."

"I haven't forgotten," Mariah said with a smile. "Don't stay late. Those can wait until Monday. Go have fun. Got a date tonight?"

Della stood and gathered the new client list up. "No dates for a while," she told her much happier looking boss. "I'm taking a computer class twice a week. If it's stuff I already know, at least the teacher is cute enough to keep me from being bored. I've decided to go for a brainy guy next time."

Mariah nodded. "Sounds like a good plan. I love plans."

"I know. I love plans too. It's one of the many things you and I have in common."

Della exited the office with a satisfied smile. Mariah stayed where she was at her desk, letting her successfulness sink in deep enough for her to start believing it again... without the reservations Dan's antagonism had caused her.

John had assured her Dan wouldn't dare bother her business anymore, not with an official reprimand on his record now about his part in the bogus court cases. He said the next black mark would effectively end Dan's career.

So at least her business was now safe. *The Perfect Date* was going to work. She felt it in her bones. She felt surer with every match she made.

Mariah touched her neck and smiled as she stood to go home to the man who'd marked her with his passion last night. John Monroe had made her sincerely believe in love and romance again. All most people wanted at the end of the day was to go home to someone they loved who loved them back. That was the essence of true happiness.

Being with the right person really was what made life perfect. There was nothing stopping her now from finding that right person for every client she took on—even when they kept insisting it was never going to happen.

Falling in love again had reminded her that 'never' wasn't nearly as long as most people thought it was.

Della stuck her head back inside the office. "John's here. He said he was picking you up for a hot date. Want me to send him back?"

Standing, Mariah shook her head as she grabbed her things. "No need. I'm ready for him."

A laughing Della gave her a thumbs up. "Great. Glad to hear it. Can I tell him you said that? I want to see that desperate lovesick look on his face."

Mariah sighed as she walked to the door. "You're going to gloat forever about being right about me and John, aren't you?"

Della's smile was wide. "Are you kidding? I'm thinking about adding it to my resume."

They were both still laughing when they nearly ran over a smirking John in the hallway. The three of them burst out chuckling at his spying.

"Still stalking me?" Mariah asked the sexy looking man who couldn't take his eyes off her.

"Yes. And I'm ready for you too," John said, pulling a smiling Mariah tight against his side.

—THE END—

KEEP READING to read an excerpt from Book 2.

NOTE FROM THE AUTHOR

Thank you for reading *Never Is A Very Long Time*!

If you enjoyed reading this book, please consider leaving a positive review or rating on the site where you purchased it. Reader reviews help my books continue to be valued by distributors/resellers and help new readers make decisions about reading them.

You are the reason I write these stories and I sincerely appreciate you!

Many thanks for your support,
~ Donna McDonald

donnamcdonaldauthor.com

Join my mailing list to hear about new releases.
donnamcdonaldauthor.com/contact

EXCERPT — NEVER SAY NEVER

ANOTHER ROMANTIC COMEDY WITH ATTITUDE

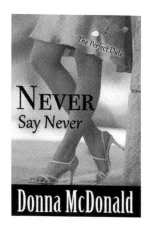

BOOK DESCRIPTION

Dating's one thing, but what's love got to do with it?

Nothing. At least not for Ann Lynx. She's fifty-three for goodness sake. She's had love. All she's in the market for these days is some fun companionship—no strings attached.

Right? Wrong.

Thanks to her pain-in-the-rear-end best friend, Georgia, she's now back on the dating scene. Add Georgia's matchmaking daughter Mariah to the mix and Ann is officially in a world of trouble—or dates—to be more accurate.

All that would be kind of doable, but her handyman's sexy too-young-for-her son is making her feel like a silly young girl. She should definitely stick to the handsome, successful, and older men that Mariah keeps throwing in her path, but she can't seem to banish the sexy Cal from her thoughts anymore than from her broken pantry.

The retired military man is very good at fixing things, and at kissing her senseless. Who's going to fix her though if Cal ends up breaking her heart?

What's love got to do with it? Maybe everything.

CHAPTER ONE

ANN WAS PULLING ON HER SWEATER WHEN THE doorbell rang. Stan was running late this morning and that meant she was now running late as well. Lateness only mattered because she was stopping by and dragging Georgia Bates along for her trip through makeover purgatory, which apparently was required before dating Mariah's rich, picky clients.

Looking through the security portal in her front door, Ann saw a set of wide shoulders and a bowed head. It wasn't Stan.

A little further down there was a tool belt settled around trim hips. Judging from the beginnings of silver streaks in his hair, she'd put the man's age somewhere in his forties. The tool belt settled on his trim hips told her the most important thing. Though he wasn't Stan, he had likely been sent by him. She'd lost so much time she had no more room to be unsettled.

"Good morning," she said cheerfully, opening the door.

"Good morning. Your son, David, asked me to come take a look at your broken pantry shelves."

"Sure. Sorry if I seem confused. I was expecting Stan Rodgers."

"Dad wasn't feeling so great today. My name is Cal. I'm Stan's son."

"Cal?" Ann repeated, inviting him inside with a sweep of her arm. There was something about the way he was built—the way he carried himself. "Oh, *Calvin*. Now I remember. You're his oldest. Didn't Stan tell me you were in the military?"

"Yes, ma'am. Command Sergeant Major in the Army until about two years ago when I retired. Mom got tired of me moping around. She suggested I come back home and help dad until I made up my mind about what to do with myself. I used to work with him every summer during high school. So here I am wearing a tool belt again. I guess it's true what they say about life coming around full circle as you get older."

"Thank you for your military service, Cal. Glad to see you're still in one piece. A sniper with a bullet retired my Marine daughter early. Glad that didn't happen to you," Ann said, leading the way down the hall to the kitchen.

"Thank you. You should probably know that I've been working part-time for David and helped out during the Christmas parade. Your daughter's a crack shot and that's no lie. I was one of Santa's elves. I helped chase the sniper down. All that running was a pretty hefty workout for an old geezer like me. Give me a boring fix-it job any day."

Ann nodded, remembering that time. "Nicholas is like my own son. He and David were college roommates and are still the best of friends. My daughter, Megan, loved that boy for years before they ever married. Thank you for whatever part you played in helping save him."

Then what he'd said about himself hit her. Ann fisted a hand on her hip and gave him a chastising look.

"*Geezer?* What in the world are you talking about? You're still in great shape for someone who's been out of the military for a couple of years."

Cal laughed at her answer instead of really responding. Ann let her gaze roam the back of him as a grinning Cal stepped into her walk-in pantry. He eyed the broken shelf with disdain and passed that same judgment on the rest of the space.

"I'll fix the one shelf if that's all you want me to fix, but honestly? I'd replace all these old wooden shelves with wire racks. They're made pretty sturdy these days. Debris falls through and you can just sweep it up from the floor. You can also vary the sizes to make the best use of your storage space."

Ann stepped inside the tiny room with him to better look around. Her wandering gaze wanted to stay on his body every time it landed on him, especially when it found him looking back. That kind of interest certainly hadn't happened to her in a while, but lustfully ogling the son of her long time handyman still seemed a bit sleazy for this early in the morning.

When his back was turned to her again, Ann firmed her mouth. "All that shelf replacing sounds expensive," she said.

"It could be," Cal agreed. "But including my labor, I'm thinking we can get by with a couple hundred dollar version. That's all you need for boxes of cereal and bottles of olive oil. Looks like you only store food in here."

"Because the shelves could never hold any more than that," Ann explained, tipping her head up to look at him.

Now that she was standing so close, she realized Cal had to be at least six feet tall. She suddenly felt tiny and had some trouble breathing around all the male pheromones he was oozing. Needing some fresh air, Ann slipped out into the kitchen again.

"If I take your suggestion, how long will it take to replace all the shelves?"

"Not long." Cal said, looking around again. "Especially not if you empty them for me while I'm out buying the new ones."

Ann shook her head. "I'd normally do it in a heartbeat, but I have an appointment that's going to last all day. I should have already left for it. Want to reschedule?"

"Not particularly. I've got other jobs to do that span the next couple of weeks. Dad was a bit backed up in his work when he got sick." Cal shrugged as he came out of the pantry. "I could probably do everything in one day, even if I have to do the moving. Can I have access to the house while you're gone for your appointment?"

"You're not planning to rob me blind, are you?"

Cal's deep throated laughter was rough and very masculine. His obvious enjoyment of her snarky reply made her smile back at him.

"Sorry. I really didn't mean that. If you ever did anything bad to me, I'd send my children after you. They're both proficient shots."

One of Cal's eyebrows lifted at the threat. His mouth

quirked at one corner. "That sort of surprises me. You look like someone who knows how to take care of herself. Will you be home for dinner?"

"I'm not sure, honey. I suggest you don't wait up," Ann teased back, fighting a grin. She crossed her arms, trying to feel as tough as she hoped she sounded. "Are you flirting with me, Calvin?"

"No. If I did that, your children wouldn't get a chance to use their weapons. My dad would skin me alive first," Cal said, grinning.

"Really?" Ann asked, surprised a bit because lots of women would be flirting right back with someone who looked like him. Wasn't that what she'd been doing? She shook her head. "That's too bad. You were about to make my day. Let me get you a key."

"Yes, ma'am. I'll be right here waiting for you."

Not sure what that meant, Ann wandered off to retrieve the spare she kept hidden in the hallway console table. Returning, she pressed it into the large masculine palm he held out to her.

"Just in case I change my mind about the flirting… is it Mrs. or Miss?" he asked.

"It's just Ann," she answered, unsure about why she'd said it quite that way.

"That's a very nice name," Cal said. "Don't worry about a thing. I've got this covered. And I'm sure I'll see you again today."

"And I'm sure I'll be back before you finish my pantry. See you later, Cal."

"Have a good day, Ann."

CHAPTER TWO

"My daughter has more money than brains. I should have known this was going to be one of those fancy places where they have to get you drunk before they work on you. The problem is that their booze is cheap and your buzz always wears off by the time you have to pay their too expensive bill."

Chuckling over her friend's complaining, Ann turned around on the sidewalk and grabbed the arm of the woman who'd gotten her into this craziness. "Don't even think about trying to run, Georgia Bates. I'm a decade younger and in better shape at the moment because you keep skipping yoga class. You promised to do this stupid makeover with me if I agreed, and you are keeping your word."

"But you know what an extremist my child is. She's not like your two. If my daughter gets her way, I'll have three more colors of hair when they get done. I already have three shades of silver. I don't need total rainbow hair with an expensive dye job I have to upkeep."

Anne grunted and held tight. "It's called highlighting and low-lighting… and it will improve your complexion. And you really, really need that haircut of yours updated. Now don't be such a big baby."

Georgia, who considered herself strong, tried to pull her arm away, but Ann Lynx had a grip of steel. "I can't believe you're so strong. No wonder your daughter joined the Marines. She must be a hoss if she takes after you."

"Lift weights and you can be like me too," Ann ordered, tugging on the arm she held.

Georgia huffed before answering. "You're just tormenting me because you don't want to do this."

Not letting go because she knew better, Ann fisted her free hand on a trim hip kept that way by exercise and not being afraid of hard work. She glared for good measure.

"Gee, you think? '*Come over for a potluck. I'm throwing a food party.*' You tricked me into this, you big old fibber."

Humor kicking in finally—mostly because of Ann's sarcasm—Georgia scrubbed a hand over her face as she laughed. "I'm sorry. It seemed like a good idea at the time. I figured it would be a lark we'd have a good laugh over."

"A lark, sure, but one I have no choice about now because my kids are ecstatic about me doing this. But don't worry, I fully intend to have the last good laugh," Ann said firmly, opening the door and shoving Georgia inside the posh interior. "I'm coming back to watch when Trudy Baxter has to deal with this makeover crap. She vowed never to put on makeup again."

Sighing because they'd been spotted immediately,

Georgia plastered a smile on her face for the attendant who took their names and marshaled them into two stylist chairs. Within the hour, they were completely foiled and sitting under dryers. Both were getting manicures and pedicures when Mariah finally came through the door and clapped her hands.

"Yay, you're here. And I see things are moving along fast. Excellent."

"Yay, we're both here…" both women said dryly, making each other laugh.

Mariah rolled her eyes. "Stop whining, you two. You're going to love the results. Manicure. Pedicure. Facial. Makeup. A new hairstyle. You two are getting the works. The image consultant will pick you up here, then it's back to the office for your interviews. I left Della practically vibrating at the thought of making your videos this afternoon."

"Why do I have to make a video? I'm not a real client," Georgia said in the flattest tone she could manage with Ann laughing from the chair beside her.

"You need to go through the whole process with Anne so Trudy won't be able to make you do it. Ann's going to give you a lot less grief. Right, Ann?"

Ann's open snickering earned her the evil eye from Georgia and a grin from Georgia's very clever daughter. She wasn't sure why Mariah was using her to get Georgia to do this, but it was a lot of fun to see her friend squirming.

"Yes. I only wanted some company to lessen the misery. Trudy would put Georgia in stilettos and a miniskirt to get even."

"Like hell," Georgia declared, rolling her eyes when the other female patrons giggled about her loud swearing.

Mariah smiled widely. "It's okay, Mom. Della and I will make the whole process today as painless as possible. Except for the eyebrow tweezing… that always hurts."

The entire salon went silent when a tall, silver-haired man in a suit came through the door. Ann noticed he walked directly to Mariah who smiled wider with every step he took towards her. His one dimple appeared just before he glanced at Georgia and grinned widely.

"Hey, Handsome," Mariah said, reaching out a hand to pat his chest.

John put a hand on her arm and kissed her cheek. "Been to the bank this morning. The house will be mine in two weeks, just before I go back to work. Still got a few routine inspections that have to be done to satisfy real estate laws."

Mariah bit her lip. "Guess you want an answer from me then, don't you?"

John glanced around. "We can talk later. I just wanted you to know things were going well."

Mariah smiled and rubbed a hand over his arm. "Good. That makes me happy. Need help moving out of your apartment?"

Huffing out a breath, John ran a hand through his hair. "Uh… about that place. It's not really mine. I just have to use it occasionally."

"I see," Mariah said, patting his arm. "Well, that makes me happy too. That place was seriously a bachelor pad."

"Great bed though, huh?" His grin was wicked as he waited for her reply.

Mariah giggled and nodded.

"Okay. So I've got to run a few more errands. Will I see you later?" John asked.

"Absolutely." Mariah went up on her toes, meeting John's lips as they came down to hers. It was a chaste kiss, but his possessive gaze never strayed from hers. The hungry look he gave her before leaving had all the women in the salon fanning themselves.

Grinning over the unexpected show, Ann reached over and poked a gawking Georgia's arm. Her friend luckily turned her way in time to catch her wink. She knew Georgia was nearly wilting in relief over her daughter's new, and promising, relationship. She would feel exactly the same if either of her adult children had gone through what Mariah had with her cheating ex-husband.

"The man has a nice butt. Bet it looks extra good in jeans," Ann whispered, gleefully giggling when Georgia rolled her eyes. What was wrong with her today? First, she was flirting with her handyman's son. Now she was making dirty jokes.

"Hey now, Ann Lynx. That's my nice butt to stare at. Keep your eyeballs to yourself," Mariah said firmly, narrowing her gaze on the two smirking older women. "I'll find you a guy of your own to ogle soon."

Giggling once more, Ann rubbed her face, which now hurt from smiling. "I didn't see your name tattooed on the man anywhere, Dr. Bates. Did you, Georgia?"

"I have no idea what you're yammering about," Georgia denied—lying for all she was worth. "But if you think John looks good, wait until you see Hollywood. The guy is your age and dates twenty-year-olds. Loaded too. He's a real looker if you can get past the 'I'm a bad little boy' thing he's perfected."

Mariah turned her narrowed gaze to her mother. "Are you talking about Dr. Colombo?"

"Some Doctor," she said sarcastically, looking directly at Ann. "Man's dumb as a box of rocks."

"*Mother*," Mariah exclaimed. "Brent is far from dumb. He's a brilliant plastic surgeon—top of his field actually."

Ann felt her freshly plucked eyebrows shoot straight up when Georgia snorted and waved that impressive factoid away with a hand now sporting brightly painted red nails.

"Big deal. That just means Hollywood *makes* those plastic females he dates. It's like he's a grown man playing with dolls. Give me a break, Mariah."

"That's a bit harsh," Ann observed, meaning it as she stared at her angry friend. Why was Georgia so angry over what some random client of Mariah's did for a living? Normally, the woman wouldn't give a good flip. "Why are you being so mean?"

"Mom likes him even though she doesn't want to," Mariah answered for her mother. "And from what Della told me, Dr. Colombo was extremely interested in Mom."

Georgia snorted as she looked away. "Hollywood was not interested in me. He was being pushy and annoying. He's as pretentious as his watch that cost more than my damn car. So no, I do not like him. He's not my type of man at all."

Ann saw Mariah nod vigorously when her mother wasn't looking. She also mouthed 'really likes him', which had her laughing behind Georgia's stiff back. But it also had her giving her friend a more considering look.

Georgia didn't date either. Trudy and Jellica both had commented that the lack of a love life was changing Georgia's personality as time went on. Her friend might benefit from having a properly interested man who wanted to soften those sharp edges. Georgia Bates was all hard shell on the outside, but inside she was a marshmallow.

"Take a taxi to the office when you're done with the image consultant. Della will meet you both downstairs with the fare," Mariah ordered. "I have clients this afternoon, but Della will take good care of you."

"That would be a miracle since Della's not even thirty yet. She can barely take care of herself," Georgia declared dryly.

Ann smiled warmly at Georgia's now frowning daughter. It was obvious Georgia was treading on thin ice with such mean teasing. "We'll be there," she promised, trying to soothe ruffled feelings.

She hoped Mariah would show her a picture of the guy Georgia was complaining about. It would be very interesting to get a look at Dr. Brentwood Colombo, the first male she'd ever seen make a dent in the emotional armor Georgia never took off.

It made her wonder what kind of man could dent hers.

CHAPTER THREE

"Hi. My name is Ann Lynx and I'm fifty-three years old. I have a Bachelor's Degree in Sociology which I've never used for any job. At the moment, I'm a semi-retired Medical Assistant who still does a little contract work when she wants. My hobbies are reading the classics, visiting with friends, and working out. I do yoga every day because I plan to be in great shape when I'm ninety."

Della smiled softly when she looked up from the camera's display. "Now tell us something unique about yourself—something only your closest, most trusted friends know about you."

Ann laughed nervously. "Okay. You might want to pause while I think about that for a minute. I'm not that interesting a person."

Her shiny red lips felt like they were covered in six layers of goo as she smiled and she wanted to rub five of them off. The feeling was highly distracting. Della and

Mariah had both approved the heavy makeup that had taken an hour for the esthetician to apply.

"Let me see. Something no one knows about me..."

Georgia cleared her throat discreetly and stepped away from the wall. She was standing behind Della and... *what in the world was the crazy woman doing now?*

Georgia's body leaned one way and then another. Luckily the blue dress with matching blue heels gave with each of her jerky movements. She stopped and glared directly at Ann, rolled her eyes, and then mimed doing a ballet pose.

Dancing! Oh yes. God... Georgia was dancing. Or trying to.

Laughing loudly at her slowness in figuring it out, Ann's embarrassed smile finally appeared for the camera. "I belly dance. Well, actually... I used to teach belly dancing. It's a great form of exercise. I never did it professionally, but my husband used to love it when I danced for him."

Her face fell as she winced. Wow. That came out without any filtering. She'd forgotten that she wasn't talking to her friends.

"Sorry. I've been a widow for a very long time and haven't dated in a while. I guess it's poor form to mention other men during your dating video, right?"

Della grinned as she shrugged. "Honesty is always good. I'll edit your answers... or ask for a retake if I need to. Don't worry about it."

Ann nodded and made herself relax again. She looked beyond Della and saw Georgia leaning against the wall once more, this time doing her best and most serene Grace Kelly impersonation.

Her friend was mercurial and intense and even a little bit unhinged at times. Why was Mariah was so calm and logical? She must have taken after her father—someone Ann had never met. She'd befriended Georgia Bates during a group grief counseling session for widows.

"Tell us a little about your perfect match, Ann. What's he look like? What does he do for a living?"

"Are you serious?" Ann asked.

Della nodded, grinning the whole time.

Ann bit her lip, then hoped she hadn't gotten lipstick on her teeth. No more smiling now, she decided. She hummed a bit as she thought. An image of a grinning Calvin Rodgers and his wide shoulders leapt into her mind. Maybe she did need to take this seriously. A long denied itch for sex was making a reappearance. Maybe she needed to find someone appropriate to scratch it.

"I've never stopped to consider what my perfect match would look like. Liking the way someone looks is so subjective. No sane woman would ever kick a man she considered handsome out of her bed... I mean... out of her life. If I have to make a list, it would be more about who he is as a person. The perfect man would be funny with me, charming to strangers, and willing to help do the dishes after dinner. Those traits may not seem glamorous by today's standards, but I know from experience they're a gift in a real relationship."

When Ann ran down, Della smiled at her. "Anything else you want to add?"

Ann took a deep breath. This was a chance to say the one thing she'd never had with any man she'd ever dated. This was probably her last and only chance to ask for what she'd like. She drew in another breath, smiling at the camera first.

"I think it would be nice to date someone who loved his work with a sincere passion. Life is far too short not to do work you absolutely love. I think being happy with how you're making a living automatically makes you a confident, happy, and very interesting person to spend time with. Is that okay to say?"

"Yes. Anything is okay. I noticed you're fairly tall for a woman. Can your perfect man be shorter than you?" Della asked.

Ann laughed at the question, because behind Della, Georgia was rolling her eyes and then her whole head. Georgia and Trudy were tall too. Jellica was the only shorty in their group and the only one who got asked out on a regular basis. They'd often talked about their non-existent dating lives and laughed at the shortage of men taller than the three of them. Though she was not a big fan of them, this situation merited a white lie or at least a slightly varnished truth.

"I've never thought about height really, but I would like a man who thought looking good for me was important. It would be hard for me to respect someone who didn't care as much as I did about how he looked."

"That's totally understandable. Any last words?" Della prompted.

Ann let a relieved sigh escape. "It's very strange to record yourself and your opinions in a video. I'm not sure how much of who I really am will be shown through this recording. Nothing really substitutes for meeting face-to-face, does it? I guess that's an old school dating sort of attitude."

Della finally stopped the recording. "It's very reasonable. You're going to find most of the men you'll meet will feel the same way as you do. Most become clients because they're tired of bar hopping and online dating sites where practically no one tells the truth. Mariah's average for finding quality dates for people is very high. She has a real gift for matching up people who have genuine things in common."

Ann nodded as she stood. "Will I get to see the video before it becomes available?"

"If you like," Della said with a sly smile, "but we're going to have to use it until we can do a second one, even if you hate it. The real purpose of the video is to show what you look like and share a bit of your personality. You came across great and not wooden at all, Ann."

Della tapped on her keyboard and then looked behind her. "Okay. You're up next, Georgia. Have a seat."

Sighing in resignation, Georgia walked around a grinning Della. Ann giggled and pinched Georgia on the arm as she passed, making her friend swear at her.

Georgia took the recording hot seat, crossing her glossed bare legs at the ankles to keep herself from bolting. Her chin lifted at a smirking Della busily adjusting the camera angle. She probably didn't want to crop off the three hundred dollar hairstyle Mariah had paid for that morning.

"Okay, Georgia. Start with your name and tell us a bit about yourself," Della ordered.

"I'm Georgia Bates. I'm sixty years old and can't believe I let my daughter talk me into making this stupid video. Don't get me wrong—Mariah is a brilliant woman and does excellent work for her clients. However, like every other adult child left with a single living parent, she likes to meddle in her mother's life—*in my life*—under the pretense of getting me to *take more chances*," Georgia finished dryly, making quote marks in the air with her red painted fingernails. "Frankly, I like my life as it is. I like myself. I do what I want, when I want, and I don't intend to stop. THAT's my idea of being happy."

Della bit the inside of her cheek to keep from laughing. "So you're not really interested in finding your perfect match? Or in dating?"

Georgia frowned and glanced off. "I didn't say that... not exactly." She dug for honesty and found a little. "It's that I've become picky about men as I've gotten older. I can't afford to play stupid games anymore. If I found someone that interested me as a man AND as a person, then of course I'd date him, or at least sleep with him. You're not meant to marry every person you feel a passing fancy about. I've seen too many widowed and divorced friends make the mistake of marrying the first person they boin..."

Ann's indrawn breath was followed by a coughing fit of shock that she pretended to fight. Georgia's glare at being interrupted had her biting her fist to stop all noise making. But where were Georgia's filters? Didn't she have any?

"As I was saying..." Georgia continued, forcing herself to smile as she stared into the damn camera. "I don't have time for games. No ego stroking. No mothering a man who can't take care of himself. There's only one reason to date someone. You date them because they're interesting, fun, and they get your engine revving. I don't see any reason not to say that plainly. Not that I recommend casual bed hopping—because I don't—but I do recommend cutting through the crap of trying to be something you're not. That kind of thing always comes out in a relationship. Am I right, Dr. Livingston?"

Della nodded. "You are exactly right, Georgia." She paused then grinned. "What's your perfect man like?"

Georgia snorted. "There's no such thing as a perfect man... or a perfect woman. There's just two flawed people trying to get to know each other and that should be good enough. Flaws make a person interesting. I do find it hard to respect a man who doesn't know what a freaking water shut off is under a toilet. Why would you ever cook dinner for someone like that? Personally, I have better things to do with my time."

Della burst out laughing and pressed the stop button. "Okay. I think we're done. Or at least I am. Both your interviews were wonderfully refreshing."

"Great," Georgia said, hearing the sarcasm tucked into the praise. "Is the torture really over now? All this nonsense has made me have to use the bathroom."

Ann glared at her friend when Della covered her mouth to stifle more laughter.

"Honestly, Georgia. Would it kill you to at least try to be a good sport? You answered like the worst she-woman man hater in the world," she chastised, only to start giggling uncontrollably at the blank look of confusion she got in response.

CHAPTER FOUR

Ann saw Stan's truck still parked in her driveway when she got home, which meant his handsome son was still at her house. She pulled her Civic into the garage and climbed out.

She told herself the only reason she hadn't changed back into her normal clothes was a lack of time. But that wasn't really the reason. The man in her pantry was. She was kind of curious to see if Cal would flirt with her again when he saw her like this.

The tiny beige kitten heels showing off the length of her full-skirted green dress made click clack sounds as she walked across the cement garage and through her tiled laundry room. The dress hit a good three inches above her knees in a length she never would have chosen alone. The image consultant Mariah worked with had insisted it suited her personality and style.

"Great timing, Ann. I just finished…" Cal's gruff voice

drifted off as he stopped and stared... and stared some more.

Ann felt her face heat under his gaze. Even her husband had never looked at her in quite that way. Cal must not be dating anyone. Otherwise, he wouldn't be acting so... deprived.

His appreciative whistle had the red creeping up and down until embarrassment covered her.

"Wow. Whatever you did today, it was worth every penny it cost. You look fantastic. Nice legs... I mean, dress."

"Thank you," Ann said politely, reaching up to nervously play with the gold butterfly charm necklace she'd worn that morning. It was the only item Della had let her keep on. "I had a complete makeover. It's part of a project I'm working on with some of my older friends. I had to make a video today."

Cal blinked a few times, but continued to stare. "I'm sure you looked great on camera."

Ann shrugged, more pleased by his comments than she was willing to admit... or show. "Pantry work finished?" she asked.

Cal nodded slowly, still dazed. "Yes, I was just putting things away. I took a few liberties with your organization. I hope you don't mind."

When he turned to walk back into the tiny space, Ann bit her bottom lip. When was the last time she'd felt so female? It had been... well, it had been ages. Maybe that was why she felt so strange around Cal.

Following him into the tiny room, Ann smiled at the new shelving with all her pantry items now neatly on display. True to his word, Cal had given her all kinds of storage. He'd even created a space big enough for the extra appliances she'd been storing on top of her refrigerator. They now sat in a tidy bottom row waiting to be needed.

"This is great—really great," Ann declared, reaching out to touch the wire racks. They did feel substantial, just like he promised they would. "Wonderful work, Cal. I'm glad I said yes to you."

She turned to see him silently staring. His intense perusal made her a bit nervous, so she did what she always did in tense situations. She laughed nervously and got sarcastic. "You're staring like you've never seen a woman in makeup before."

Cal gave a man grunt that had her ducking her head in embarrassment for being so bold with him.

"Been a while since I've seen one who looked quite as good as you do at the moment. I thought you looked cute this morning…"

"*Cute?*" Ann repeated, laughing at his words. Could a woman over fifty still be cute? Wasn't there an age limit on that kind of description?

"… but your new look is a magical transformation," Cal declared, pausing to look her up and down. "I'm wishing like hell I had on my dress uniform so I could ask you out to dinner. A woman who looks as good as you do right now needs to go out and be shown off."

Ann swallowed with difficulty because there was now an emotional lump in her throat. How did Cal keep throwing her so off balance? "If I'm not responding glibly enough, it's because I'm not used to hearing so many compliments in a single day. You exceeded my limit in the last ten minutes."

Cal chuckled, then grinned at her. He reached out, took her hand, and lifted her knuckles to his lips. The feel of his warm mouth against her skin sent a shiver down her spine.

He kept his gaze on her knuckles as he spoke. "I haven't felt like dating much in the last couple of years, so I'm out of practice. Do you think we could maybe have dinner for real sometime?"

Ann opened her mouth to tell him they couldn't do that, but the refusal refused to come out of her mouth. What did finally emerge was shocking.

"Are you in a hurry to get home this evening? I can offer you some leftover beef stew with spicy cornbread. One of my friends is a retired chef and she taught me the recipe. It's really good as long as you eat it hot."

Cal grinned, rubbing a thumb over her knuckles. He squeezed her hand tighter as he answered. "Just so I know I'm not imagining this… you want me to stay tonight?"

"For dinner, Cal. That's all I'm offering," Ann said softly. "I just…"

Cal chuckled, squeezed her hand again, and then quickly released it. "I'd love to eat with you. Let me put the rest of the pantry stuff away."

Ann nodded. She looked down at herself. "Do you mind if I change out of this outfit?"

Grinning, Cal shook his head. "Are you kidding? I can't wait to see what you pick to wear next. It's been fun watching you change clothes all day."

"I usually just wear my yoga clothes around the house."

His masculine groan set her face on fire. She swallowed her nervousness and spoke the rest of her thoughts. "And I swear I don't make a habit of inviting strange men to hang around for meals."

"Glad to hear I'm your exception," Cal said. "And I won't tell my father about this, if you won't."

His teasing about Stan made her giggle. "How old are you, Cal? Seventeen?"

"Yes... two and a half times that."

Ann studied the ceiling for a moment trying to do the math in her head. Cal's laughter had her looking back at him.

"I'm forty-three," he supplied. "I've been divorced over a decade and have two daughters. One is in college. The other graduates high school in a year."

Ann nodded, smiling softly in sympathy. "Divorce can be hard. My friend's daughter just went through a nasty one. It's hard on the whole family."

Cal nodded and then shrugged. "Like most military men, I was gone a lot. Not every woman can handle that kind of life. My ex discovered she couldn't. We divorced and I never remarried, not even after she did. What's most important is that the girls and I are fine. Their stepfather is a decent guy. They live outside of Dayton, and when we're together, we all get along. Things could be much, much worse than I have it."

Ann nodded in agreement. "I've always counted my blessings that my marriage was as strong as it was. Can you believe that I've never lived anywhere else in my life but Norwood? The Cincinnati area is all I know. And I'm fifty-three."

"You're over fifty? Wow, you're my first older woman," Cal teased.

"I'm not actually your anything," Ann replied haughtily, but the effect was spoiled by the corner of her mouth twitching.

Cal grinned at her and dropped his gaze to her legs. When it lifted, the look in his eyes made every nerve ending flutter inside her.

"*Yet,* Ann… you're not my anything *yet*. Isn't that is a such great word?"

Cal then made a shooing motion at her with his hands. The action sent her into giggles as she backed out of the pantry to let him pass by her.

"I don't mean to be rude, but I have to finish this job. I've got a hot date tonight with a woman in yoga clothes. I don't want to keep her waiting too long."

ANN FILLED CAL'S BOWL A SECOND TIME, THEN brought the rest of the pan to the table. The way he was eating, she knew he'd be able to finish it all. She set the remaining stew close to him, pushing the pan with the remainder of Trudy's special cornbread closer as well.

Fetching two more beers from the refrigerator, she set one by his plate and opened the other for herself. Some liked their wine—and she liked a glass now and again—but she loved imported beer and always kept a cold six pack on hand. It was a special treat for her.

Ann brought one leg up into her chair and curved her arm around her knee. This was her favorite way to sit. It made her feel like things were normal despite her sexy, masculine, and very distracting company.

"Finish the rest of the stew if you can. I've had all I want of it and the rest will only get tossed later," she told him.

Nodding absently, Cal watched every move she made as she wiggled and got more comfortable. He was eating the whole time he stared at her. The man looked the way she imagined a hungry wolf would look plowing through his first meal after nearly starving. Didn't anyone ever feed him?

"You keep staring at me, Cal. I know I scrubbed those six layers of red lipstick off before I started cooking."

"That's not it," he said.

Ann giggled. "Never seen a woman drink two beers before?" She knew her sass had gotten her into trouble again when his eyes narrowed.

"I've never seen a woman drink two beers who looks as good as you do. Unless you're wearing one of those all over make-me-look-skinny things under your clothes. Are you?"

Ann rolled her eyes. "That was not a polite question, you know."

Cal guiltily moved his stare to the remainder of his stew. "I guess now you know why I'm still single after all this time."

Ann snickered over his social discomfort and took another drink of her beer. She hadn't meant to make him feel bad.

"If you must know… I'm not wearing anything at all under my clothes. I work out for the sole purpose of being about to eat and drink anything I want. You have to do that at my age when you have friends who cook better than you do. God save me from anyone who hates carbs. I hate those people, don't you?"

Cal's spoon clattered to his bowl as it fell, and she laughed at his flinching over it.

"What's wrong now?" she asked, pretending to be exasperated.

"Sorry. I'm a guy. All I heard was the nothing-under-your-clothes part of your speech."

She laughed harder when Cal lifted his already opened beer and drank the remaining one-third of it before stopping.

"I'm sorry if I'm embarrassed you with my frankness," Ann said, not really meaning the apology... and she figured they both knew it.

The truth was she was enjoying the masculine attention Cal was showing her. It had been a very long time since she'd had male company across her dinner table. Not even David ate with her very often. Her son was too busy running his business. Her daughter, Megan, hovered and worried when she came by. Children could never really replace the company of a spouse. On some level, Ann supposed her children finally understood that after finding their own life partners.

Cal shook his head as he sipped from the fresh beer. "I'm not embarrassed at all—not by anything you say. I just feel like I've been hit by a train I didn't see coming. Today has been very surprising for me."

Ann laughed. "What in the world does that mean?"

"I like you, Ann... and I'd like..." he paused, looking guilty again. "I'd like to like you even more if you'd let me."

Giggling, Ann felt her face flame at his poor innuendo. "Are you trying to say you'd like to sleep with me without actually saying it?"

Cal widened his eyes and took a big bite of cold cornbread to keep from replying.

"It's okay, Cal. You're my first bold move in about thirty years. I feel the tug between us too, but I don't do that sort of thing, not even with random handsome men I invite to dinner in a moment of weakness."

Cal nodded. "You know... I'm both relieved and disappointed. Never felt that combination before. It's an interesting feeling. Yet also somehow appropriate. Strange."

Ann smiled at his candid reaction. "I think it's just been this day. My friend's daughter runs this very expensive dating service. Somehow I got talked into becoming a client—not a real one, mind you—just enough of one to get my children to quit worrying about me being alone. I've been a widow for close to a decade now and haven't really dated much. Truthfully? I haven't really wanted to."

Cal swallowed his food, took a drink, and then brought his gaze to hers. "So..." he waved a hand at her, "you got all dolled up today to join a dating service to make David and Megan think you were really dating again?"

Ann sighed and nodded. "Yes. And please don't rat me out to them. I thought I'd hate the whole process. I left this morning intending to hate the makeover part. But the truth is... I didn't hate it. When I came home and you reacted so..."

"Like a normal guy who got blown away when he saw a beautiful woman standing two feet away from him looking like she needed to be kissed?" Cal prompted.

DONNA MCDONALD

Ann grinned and nodded again. "Yes. What can I say? It's been a very long time. It was nice to feel pretty again. That's why I asked you to stay for dinner. Do you understand?"

Cal nodded. "I do. But you were also pretty this morning before you did anything fancy to yourself. I couldn't stop thinking about you all day. The rest with you all fixed up... it was like a fantasy coming to life. Your new hairstyle is very flattering by the way, but I've never known how to say anything like that to a woman without her cringing."

"Well, I'm not cringing. I'm flattered. It's very sweet of you to tell me, Cal."

Cal frowned. "Not really as sweet as you think. I'm just being honest. Why can't you believe I find you sexy?"

"Oh, I do," Ann said, sighing around her beer. "I just don't know what to do about it. Getting churned up about how I look and caring about you noticing... that's all like trying to get in touch with a part of myself I haven't seen in a while."

"If you don't know what to do with me and my interest, it really has been a long time for you," Cal joked.

Giggling over his smirk, Ann sobered enough to take the last drink of her beer. "I appreciate your company and your flirting. It was a nice pretend date for me. I haven't spent this much time with a man other than my son in literally years. I hope that's another confidence you'll keep."

Cal finished his beer, stood, and carried his dishes to the sink. "Can I help you clean up?"

The woman in her melted a little... and Cal hadn't seen the video she'd made today. He was being considerate, but that didn't make him meant for her. He was too much younger and too much... male. Yes, that was it. Sexual heat rolled off him whenever she got close. Cal was far too male for a woman who'd been without one for such a long time. Today was just a pleasant, unexpected interlude in both their lives.

"There's only a few things to wash, Cal. I can get them. I'm sure you're tired after working all day. You need to get home."

Tearing her gaze from his now sad one, Ann rose from her seat and fetched the check she'd written out to Stan's business earlier. She handed it over after Cal collected the tool belt he'd hung from one of new racks in the pantry.

She walked him to her front door, opening it to let him leave. Cal stopped and turned to her.

"This has been the best day I've had since I got out of the military. Can I kiss you goodnight?" he asked.

Letting a long nervous breath escape the confines of her tight chest, Ann reluctantly nodded. Cal's lips touched hers slowly, the warmth of his kiss seeping into every cell as his mouth slid confidently across hers. She heard a soulful moan, but wasn't sure which of them made it.

A strong hand slipped around her waist, then fell to her backside. Cal used it to drag her whole body up against the front of his. Their kiss changed instantly from something innocent to something needy and desperate, complete with mutual writhing against each other trying to appease the longing to connect.

It was too wonderful for words. It was also too much too fast.

Using a now trembling hand, Ann gently pushed their

bodies apart. She also took a step back. It was the only way she could breathe.

"I don't care about our differences. Will you at least think about giving this attraction we have a chance?" Cal whispered.

Ann closed her eyes, trying to think of an honest reply that wouldn't hurt his feelings. She only opened them when she heard a truck starting. She watched Cal smile and wave before driving away.

Feeling lonely now and not liking it at all, Ann closed the door and tried to forget her strange, strange day.

~

Want the rest of the story?
www.donnamcdonaldauthor.com/never-say-never

SPECIAL LOOK AT BOOK 3

** GEORGIA AND BRENT **

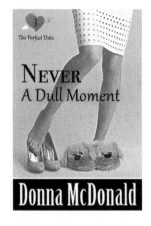

What could she possibly have in common with a man whose watch costs more than her car?

Georgia may be slowing down a bit at sixty, but she isn't stupid yet. The idea of her genuinely dating Dr. Brentwood Colombo, aka Hollywood when he poses in her doorway... well, that's just totally insane.

Where is her dignity? Where is her pride? How did she let her snickering friends dare her into giving him a chance? And where is the kind, caring daughter she raised?

Mariah's been replaced with an evil version who keeps insisting she give the womanizing plastic surgeon who dates twenty-year-olds a fair chance. A fair chance at what, Georgia wonders? Breaking her heart?

No, thank you. She would rather keep her womanly dignity than see it trampled under Hollywood's expensive, polished shoes.

Now if he'd just stop talking about her perfect, perfect breasts, she might forget about him completely.

For More Information About This Title Visit…
www.donnamcdonaldauthor.com/never-a-dull-moment

OTHER BOOKS BY THIS AUTHOR

The Perfect Date Series
Never Is A Very Long Time
Never Say Never
Never A Dull Moment
Never Ever Satisfied
Never Be Her Hero
Never Try To Explain
Never Look Back
Never Ever Been Better
Never Too Old To Date

Never Too Late Series
Dating A Cougar
Dating Dr. Notorious
Dating A Saint
Dating A Metro Man
Dating A Silver Fox
Dating A Cougar II

OTHER BOOKS BY THIS AUTHOR

Dating A Pro

Art Of Love Series
Carved In Stone
Created In Fire
Captured In Ink
Commissioned In White
Covered In Paint
Carved In Wood

Non-Series Books
The Wrong Todd
SEALed For Life
A Secret Dare
Saving Santa
Mistletoe Madness
No ELFing Way

ABOUT THE AUTHOR

USA Today Bestselling Author, Donna McDonald, published her first novel in March of 2011. Many multi-genre novels later, she admits to living her own happily ever after as a full-time author. Addicted to making readers laugh, she includes a good dose of romantic comedy in every book.

Contact Donna...
www.donnamcdonaldauthor.com
email@donnamcdonaldauthor.com

Made in the USA
Columbia, SC
29 August 2023